Lost Creek

R.j Ruud

ISBN-10: 0-9998890-0-1
ISBN-13: 978-0-9998890-0-8

The proper function of man is to live, not to exist. I shall not waste my days in trying to prolong them. I shall use my time.

—Jack London

CHAPTER 1

It's been nearly a year since I stumbled upon this strange mountain town. I was a completely different person when I first arrived. I looked young and I felt old. I wore the latest styles. I cut my hair regularly. I showered and shaved, daily. Today, my own mother wouldn't recognize me. And not a single person that knew the old me would ever believe I was capable of killing seven people.

I was just your average early-thirties working professional before a certified letter led me to Lost Creek, Colorado. I went to college after high school. I graduated with a computer sciences degree. I didn't particularly like computers, I really didn't know what I liked, but my high school guidance counselor told me there was a large demand in the field. I was hired right out of college at a website design firm in Minneapolis. Sitting in front of a computer was not my idea of a good time, but the money was good. I bought my first home in 2007. It was much more than I needed. It was a three-bedroom house on Lake Minnetonka. But my agent said I could sell it at any time and make a profit. And then the market crashed. I tried to sell the house, but that same agent told me the property was only worth half of what I owed. I had to trade my brand-new cherry-red Audi A4 for a rusted-out Honda Accord with over 200,000 miles. I was waiting tables at night and delivering newspapers in the early morning when the foreclosure notices started piling up.

I lost my home in the spring of 2009 and had to move back in with my father in northern Minnesota. I was just about to let myself settle for the dreaded role of carpenter for my father's construction company, which I had desperately gone to college to avoid, when I received the letter that would change my life. Assuming it was just another nasty letter from the bank's lawyer, I tossed it on the pile. I probably would have never read it had Pops not pointed out that, unlike the others, it was from Colorado. And, unlike the others, this lawyer's letter promised to give me a home. It said I had been named as the only benefactor of the Martin Johansson estate. I was sure it was a hoax. I didn't know Martin Johansson. I didn't know any Johanssons. I asked Pops; he said there were no Johanssons on his side of the tree. I called my mother — she divorced Pops before my senior year — she said there were no Johanssons on her side. I was certain, as was my entire family, that the letter was a scam. I Googled the lawyer's name — he didn't even have a website. But the thought of pounding nails beside my brother and father for the rest of my life made me grasp for any possibility. I even considered the foolish notion of the long-lost rich uncle. In fact, I think it was that very thought that made me Google the lawyer's address. The directions indicated it would take me fifteen hours and thirty-three minutes to get there. Pops and my brother were laughing at me as I pulled out of the driveway in my rusty old Honda. Their intent was to ridicule until I realized I should stay, but it only pushed me away.

It took over sixteen hours before I spotted the Rocky Mountains. Her peaks cut a jagged horizon into the brilliant blue sky, from north to south, as far as the eye could see. Her magnificence only climbed higher as I approached the city. The skyscrapers of downtown were outhouses in her shadow by the time my GPS warned me that I was ten minutes from my destination.

I didn't notice how bad I smelled until I sat before the lawyer's desk. After driving straight through to save money, the smell of gas station sandwiches, stale soda, greasy hair and body odor quickly overpowered the vanilla-leather smell of the office. I had just come to realize the level of my stench when an old-timer hobbled in and took a seat at the head of the desk. His cowboy boots were scuffed. His blue jeans were stained and faded. His brown corduroy sport coat only hung on his chair for extremely important occasions. He looked like no lawyer I had ever seen. I was sure he was going to try to rope me into some sort of real estate scam. He assured me all I had to do was give my signature and I would be the proud owner of a home on a hundred acres in the Rocky Mountains — it would cost me nothing. I kept waiting for the catch. It never came.

"Why me?" I asked as the lawyer handed me the keys.

"Can't say," he said with a disconcerting smirk.

My GPS said my destination was an hour away. I was so exhausted, renting a room and getting a few hours of sleep was seriously contemplated. If not for my dwindling savings — filling the tank across the country consumed much more than anticipated — I'm certain I could've accommodated. But the thought of a free place to stay was all I needed to be motivated. I let my GPS lead me through town and followed her voice onto Peak to Peak Highway. It was like no road I had ever traveled. Steep rocky cliffs climbed thousands of feet toward the sky on either side. The road followed a river that had been carving out that gorge for a million years. IN CASE OF FLOOD CLIMB TO SAFETY read the signs. The curves were so sharp I thought I would sail over the edge at twenty-five miles per hour. The climb was so steep my rusty old Honda could hardly manage. WATCH FOR FALLING ROCKS was the sign that really scared me. All I could picture was roaring around a blind corner, with a line of angry locals behind me, only to see a boulder the size of a Volkswagen sitting in the middle of the road. There would be nothing you could do. A sheer rock cliff was no more than six inches from the mirror on the passenger's side. A thousand-foot drop into the river loomed on the other. Not to mention the traffic that raced down the hill at ninety miles an hour in the opposite lane.

My poor little Honda was barely shuddering up the mountain when my eyes first spotted Black Hawk. I was certain I was hallucinating. There, in the middle of nowhere, sandwiched in a canyon between two rocky cliffs, was a miniature Las Vegas. Dozens of casinos lined the street. Monstrous skyscrapers climbed higher than the cliffs. I had already been driving for well over an hour, but my GPS insisted I continue to climb. Ten minutes past the last casino, I was driving on top of the world. The keenest of eyes could surely see both coasts from such heights. Then the road dropped. I raced down the other side of the mountain, past rundown ranches and towns that never had a chance. My brakes were squealing and shuddering by the time I dropped into Lost Creek.

The town was nothing more than a few homes scattered about the surrounding hills and a big red barn along the highway. I would later learn that the big red barn was the Wagon Wheel Saloon. I wouldn't have guessed it to be a town had my GPS not warned me of my impending left turn onto Lost Creek Canyon Road.

Lost Creek Canyon Road is a washboard of an old dirt road — I thought the wheels of the Accord were going to rattle right off. Had the scenery not been so breathtaking, I'm sure I would have turned around. Sprawling green fields full of grazing cattle spread to rocky cliffs on either side. Little log ranch homes rested where the fields began to climb. The rushing Lost Creek River slithered up the valley. I was to follow Lost Creek Canyon Road for 3.2 miles. I did. I was to then turn left onto Lost Creek Trail. There wasn't a road in sight. I continued down Lost Creek Canyon for another mile without spotting a single road on the left. I did find the Lost Creek Tavern on the right.

I have never felt so lost and out of place as I did the moment I stepped through that creaky tavern door. And I've felt like an outsider my whole life. Conceived in Denver, born in Missouri, moved to Minneapolis before I was one, my family never lived anywhere long enough to settle. Pops was a carpenter and my folks hopped from city to city, following the sprawling suburbs. I spent most of my childhood, what I can remember of it anyway, jumping from school to school as my father built the suburbs of Minneapolis. I never spent more than a single year in the same school until high school. But not one of those horrible first-day-in-a-new-school days could compare to the "you don't belong here" feeling I got when I saw two crusty hillbillies turn to stare at me as the tavern door slammed. From the expressions on their faces, I knew I looked just as strange to them as they did to me. Even after almost eighteen hours on the road, I looked clean compared to them. I was wearing tennis shoes, shorts, and a button-up short-sleeved shirt. They were wearing work boots, heavy pants, and tattered flannels. My hair was short and styled. Their hair was long and scraggly.

"You lost, boy?" the rugged old bartender grumbled, as he stepped behind the bar with a rattling rack of glasses.

"Don't many folk that turn up lost in the Creek ever turn up again," chuckled the hillbilly at the far end of the bar. All three of them rolled with laughter. I turned for the door, expecting to be shot in the back as I reached for the knob.

"They're just messin' with ya," yelled the hillbilly closest to the door, the one with the green and blue flannel over camouflage pants. "Where you need to get?"

"107 Lost Creek Trail," I sputtered as I stared at the giant knife hanging from his belt.

"Martin's place?"

"I guess. My GPS said to turn a mile back, but…"

The hillbillies erupted with laughter.

"GPS!?" cried the bartender. "That shit don't work up here."

"Gotta go 'bout a mile further," the man with the giant knife explained. "Look fer the old lodge pole that was struck by lightning on yer right. Lost Creek Trail is on the left. Martin's driveway's 'bout a hundred yards up, on the left. Can't miss it."

Lost Creek Trail was almost exactly a mile past the bar, right after the lightning-stricken lodge pole. And it climbed straight up. Not only did it climb straight up, but it was so washed out that the ruts were a good two feet deep. My muffler was torn off and lying on the road behind me after twenty yards. If I could have possibly turned around on that narrow road, I would have.

The driveway was on the left, just like the hillbilly said. It was barely wider than the car and straight up.

I can't possibly describe the look of disappointment that came over my face when I climbed the last steep pitch of the driveway to see my new "home." It was nothing more than a little log shack. The logs were never even peeled before they were stacked to form the walls. The bark was long ago blackened by weather and flaking. The roof was framed with two-inch saplings, covered with rusty corrugated steel pipe that had been bent flat. My father's toolshed was bigger than the entire shack. My living room in Minnetonka was twice the size. But the thought of the cash I would get from selling the hundred acres quickly turned my thoughts to getting a good night's sleep. I was going to head straight to the nearest Realtor in the morning and put the place up for sale. I couldn't wait to finally take a shower as I lugged my suitcase up the rickety old stairs and onto the porch.

I was given a set of keys with the deed — I still have no idea what they're for. There was no lock on the front door. Only a stick nailed with a single nail, so it could swivel, held the door from blowing open. Dust flew when I kicked open the door. Spiderwebs hung from every surface. A rusty fifty-gallon barrel sat in the middle of the floor with a slinky of tubing running to the ceiling — I would later learn that it was my only source of heat. Against the opposite wall was a straw-filled mattress perched atop a bedframe made of logs. Next to the door was a big makeshift bookshelf with one solitary book set upon its shelves. At the back of the room was a pipe coming out of the floor with a five-gallon pail hanging off the hand pump — my only source of water. And a thick layer of dust covered every dirty inch. There was no electricity. There was no shower. There wasn't even a bathroom — I slept in the car the first night.

I was up with the sun the following morning. With an empty stomach, I rumbled the mufflerless Accord down the mountain and into Golden Realty.

"Price it to sell," I told the agent.

"You'll be lucky to give that property away, honey," she

responded.

We settled on putting it on the market for half of what such acreage sold for a year prior. The next stop was the grocery store for cleaning supplies and food that didn't need refrigeration. I figured a box of dry cereal, a few pouches of jerky, peanut butter, jelly, and a loaf of bread would do — I was going to hit the road for Minnesota as soon as I got the shack cleaned.

The weather was perfect when I got back to the shack. The sun was high and hot. Wispy white clouds danced across the brilliant blue mountain sky. Birds were singing in every tree. But I didn't have time for all that. My only concern was cleaning. That's when I met Blue, the strangest-looking dog I have ever seen. He stormed out of the rubber doggy flap in the door with a rumbling growl just as I reached the top step of the rickety stairs that climbed to the porch. His coat was black, flickered with silvery wisps that made him look an eerie shade of blue. His shoulders and hindquarters were rippled with tense, twitching muscles, but his ribs and spine seemed about to poke right through his skin. And his sharp eyes glared right through me with sinister intent — I was to be his next meal.

"Go on!" I shook my fist.

His response was a deep and rumbling growl from a mouthful of bright white fangs. I thought I could just step towards him and he would back down, but that damn dog seemed to know exactly what I was thinking. Before I even attempted my first step, the dog hunched and the fur on his back bristled into a mohawk. I've always been good with dogs, but that rabid bastard wasn't falling for any of my tricks. His eyes actually laughed at me when I tried to lure him off the porch by throwing a stick. It wasn't until I thought to bribe him with jerky that I got him to budge. It took one whole pouch, but I was finally able to lure him away from the door long enough to sneak in and block the doggy door with the bookshelf. And the joke was on me — that damn dog got the shits from the jerky and crapped all over every square inch of the porch, which I didn't find until stepping in it the following morning.

I spent the next two days scrubbing every inch of the dusty

shack with freezing cold water from the hand pump. And that angry blue dog was on my heels the whole time. He watched every move I made to make sure I didn't disturb anything he considered sacred. I had never seen a dog with such vivid expressions. I could tell exactly what he was thinking by the look on his face. At the time I was certain that, had I not been feeding him, he would have torn off my face. Looking back, though, I'm pretty sure Blue knew something I would have never even considered.

During the daylight hours, while cleaning, I rarely thought about my Minnesota money troubles. It was a welcome distraction — therapeutic, almost. Come nightfall, the darkness sent my mind wandering. It's amazing just how far the mind can roam without modern distractions like television, Internet, electricity, and cell phones — there wasn't even cell service up here. You wouldn't believe how early it got dark with no light switch to flip — especially when there was only one smoke-hazed window. The early darkness was the hardest adjustment. Hanging from a log rafter in the middle of the shack was an old kerosene lantern that helped with the darkness factor — once I finally learned how to light it. But the eerie screams of the mountain's wild always followed the setting sun. It started with one lone yip in the far distance. Two or three coyotes were quick to yip back. Suddenly hundreds of yipping and hollering coyotes had the shack surrounded. Some nights they sounded like they were right outside the door. It was on one of those nights that Blue showed me how to properly block the doggy door. The claws of angry coyotes were click-clacking against the wood floor of the porch, right outside the door. I was hiding under the covers by that point. But Blue kept nudging me and trying to lead me to the door. At first, I thought he was trying to get me to go out there. Then he pawed at a board behind the bookshelf. It wasn't until he got ahold of it with his teeth and brought it back and forth between me and the door that I realized I was supposed to slide the little square chuck of paneling into the channel around the doggy door, blocking anything from getting into the shack. I slept somewhat easier after that. But there are beasts far bigger than coyotes in these woods.

It must have been the second or third night that I awoke to the most blood-curdling bellow you can possibly imagine. It was right in the back yard. I could tell from the deep throaty bugle that the beast was bigger than a Buick. And his reinforcements were bugling back from the ridge to the north. I thought I was a goner that night. There was no way I was getting back to sleep. I finally grabbed the one lonely book from the bookshelf, thinking that reading would take my mind off the bellowing and help me fall asleep. I was never much of a reader before Lost Creek — I don't think I had ever read a single book that wasn't assigned for some class. The book was thick — over a thousand pages. I was relieved to find it was full of short stories. It was *The Collected Jack London*. The first story, "To Build a Fire," took me right out of the shack and dropped me on the Yukon Trail, where my worries were quickly turned from the bellowing outside to freezing to death. I fell sound asleep two pages into the second story, "An Odyssey of the North." I would later learn the bellowing was only the cry of the harmless elk.

The only nights that didn't scream with strange beasts were the nights of the howling wind. And those were the eeriest of all nights. The wind alone could drive a man mad up here. It blew up out of nowhere at a hundred miles per hour. The whole shack creaked and shifted from the gusts. The roof wailed like it was going to be ripped right off. But it was the constant light wind that could really drive you crazy as it whistled through the cracks and rattled the old single-pane window.

The bathroom situation also took some getting used to — there wasn't one. There was an outhouse just behind the shack, but the thought of some critter crawling up and biting my ass was a hard one to get past. I quickly trained my body not to have to go after dark — especially number two. But worse than that, there was no shower. (I shouldn't say there wasn't a shower; I just didn't know that the five-gallon bucket with little holes drilled in the bottom that hung from the ceiling in the back corner of the shack *was* the shower.) If I boiled water in the tea kettle over the barrel stove, I could fill a five-gallon bucket in just under an hour. Once full, I had to strip down, climb onto a little log bench carrying a five-gallon bucket full of hot water, and pour it into the bucket hanging from the ceiling. A full bucket lasted about three minutes. The floor under the bucket was covered with corrugated steel that slanted to the corner where a trough carries the water to a pipe that poured right out the back corner of the shack. There was a little sliding trap door that blocked the pipe to keep little critters and the cold night drafts from blowing in — I didn't learn that until I flooded the shack floor during my first shower attempt. Shaving was impossible. The "mirror" was nothing more than a shiny square of metal nailed to the wall next to the bucket. The reflection was dull and blurry with no definition. My face was a bloody mess after my first attempt at shaving. I've been growing a beard ever since.

Such hardships are highly exaggerated when the stomach is rumbling. Eating properly, without the luxury of refrigeration and electricity, was nearly impossible. By the third morning, I was so hungry for a cooked meal I attempted to return to the Lost Creek Tavern. I changed into the dirty clothes that I had been wearing to clean the shack and got there just before the doors opened at 11:00 a.m. I thought I could get in and out before the local hillbillies arrived. I was wrong. Two old hillbillies were waiting for the door to open and glaring at me as I slowly drove past. I didn't dare stop. The beer lights were just starting to flicker in the windows of the Wagon Wheel as I approached the intersection of Peak to Peak Highway. The sign said they were open for lunch. I never considered it. Instead, I turned left onto Peak to Peak in search of something a bit more civilized. Five curvy downhill miles later, I found myself in Nederland, the strangest town I've ever seen. Instead of angry old hillbillies, the town was teeming with cheery, longhaired hippies. I ate lunch and dinner at a little brewery every day for the rest of the week. I had decided I should postpone my return trip to Minnesota for a few weeks in case the property sold right away — I didn't want to have to come back to sign papers, I told myself. And my savings quickly dwindled. Between the cost of eating out every day and all the gas the Accord guzzled climbing back up the hill to Lost Creek, I figured I would be completely broke in less than a month.

The second week, I stocked up on jerky, fruit, and dry cereal at the local market in Nederland. I even bought a bag of dog food for that damn Blue dog — which he wouldn't touch. Looking back, I think that was the week I fell in love with this strange place. I think it was the natural beauty and its ability to completely drown out the stress and confusion of this bustling life that initially addicted me. The shack is nestled into the side of a mountain that climbs a thousand feet into the bright blue sky behind. The porch looks across a valley cut by a rolling river, and on to another mountain range that cuts a jagged horizon to the north. I spent every daylight hour of that week sitting on the porch, staring into the beautiful solitude. The clouds alone were enough to capture a whole day's attention. Maybe I was just willing to do anything to prolong the inevitable return trip to Minnesota, where I would be forced to settle into the dreadful carpenter's life. Whatever the case, I figured I could last until the end of August if I only burned gas going down the hill and back once a week for supplies and only bought the cheapest brands.

It wasn't until the third week that I decided to venture off the porch. Blue and I had grown to tolerate each other, as long as I didn't try to pet him, and I fed him a fair portion of whatever I was eating — except for fruit or vegetables, which he would spit right out — but we were nowhere near friends. Then I wandered into the backyard after our morning helping of dry cereal. Blue didn't know what to do. He stood on the porch and whined until I was out of sight. Thirty seconds later, he was nipping at my heels.

Martin's spread was substantial. It was beautiful. Dark and eerie groves of mossy pines climbed the hill until the air became too thin. Wandering under their dark cover transported me to a simpler time. Listening to the rustling aspens killed all chatter of the brain. I think that's when Blue finally decided I was alright. We hiked around the property for hours that day. Blue would prance along in front of me, constantly looking back to make sure I was following him. If I happened to veer off from his path and cross some imaginary line, he would quickly circle back and nudge me until I was back on track. It took me the whole week to figure out that he was showing me the property lines. Up to that point, I thought I had been training him. But it was obvious that he was training me. I could have set a watch by the time he pawed at the doggy door every morning so I would let him out to do his business. He would always return just in time to share handfuls of dry cereal on the porch as the sun rose over the valley to the east. As soon as the food was gone, Blue would nudge my thigh with his nose and then jump off the porch. If I didn't follow, he would jump back on the porch, circle around my legs, and then jump back off the porch and stare at me until I followed him. Soon we were hiking all day. I would pack a backpack full of food and water and we wouldn't return to the shack until sunset. We covered every square inch of the property that week.

Then Blue crossed the line. He had me so well-trained on the property lines, I almost didn't follow. Especially when I saw the NO TRESPASSING signs nailed to every other tree along the river. I even stopped at one point, looking at one of the signs with great concern, but Blue's eyes assured me that everything would be okay. So, I followed Blue upstream for almost an hour until we came across some railroad tracks that followed the river. My feet were throbbing and I was drenched with sweat when Blue splashed across the river and went charging up the rocky cliff on the other side. I was too exhausted to follow. But that damn dog was a persistent bastard. As soon as I sat down at the edge of the river and opened my pack, he started barking incessantly. That was the first time I had ever heard him bark. Even his bark was like no other. Realizing he would not stop until I obeyed, I followed. It was a steep climb up the rocky mountainside. I was huffing and puffing when I finally found Blue standing on the edge of a cliff that dropped a thousand feet straight down. It was the perfect perch that overlooked the entire valley. It was a much better spot for lunch than my rock at the edge of the river. And Blue smiled the biggest "I told you so" smile you have ever seen. "Yeah, yeah," I said as I poured a pile of cereal on the rocks at Blue's feet. Yeah, I was talking to the dog after the first few days. Going so many days without speaking to another human being can really make a guy crave conversation.

Anyway, I was just about to toss back a handful of cereal when the steamy whistle of a locomotive screamed around the bend. Then a bright yellow engine roared into the valley with a long line of cars heaped with deep black coal. I felt like I had traveled back in time. As my eyes followed the engine, I caught Blue looking up at me to catch my reaction. And I'm pretty sure I was grinning ear to ear. All I know is Blue turned to face the train, sat, and smiled as we watched the whole line pass. When the last car was gone around the bend, Blue was ready to lead me on. I couldn't do it. My whole body was sore when I stood up after lunch. My lungs were burning for oxygen. And Blue didn't push it; he knew I had had enough. So, he led me home.

We hiked further and further each day. We left earlier and earlier each morning. Some days we would stop to watch the train; some days we would continue up the river. I think Blue somehow knew the train schedule. One day, a few weeks into our hikes, the forest along the river opened to reveal an old train tunnel that dived right into the side of the Continental Divide. We arrived just in time to watch the big yellow coal train dive into the tunnel. The next two days, we continued past the tunnel on a trail that climbed the very mountain that the tunnel cut through. I have never seen such beautiful wilderness. The trail followed a rushing river up the mountain. Old log cabins, having long ago succumbed to the years and the weather, were scattered throughout the forest on the lower half of the trail. Strange pine groves, where all the trees were covered with webs of spooky green moss, followed the river. About an hour past the tunnel, the trail began to climb straight up. I couldn't make the climb. Blue knew. I could tell he was disappointed, but he knew, and he turned around.

I conquered the trail the following day. It was a Friday. I didn't know it at the time, but I realized the next day. We didn't see a single soul the first two days on the trail. I couldn't figure why the trail was even there. I imagined it was some sort of horse trail left over from the Cowboys and Indians days. Anyway, we made it to Crater Lake on the second day. It was the most beautiful body of water I had ever seen. And growing up in Minnesota, I've seen a lot of water. Even the fact that Crater Lake would probably be considered a pond in Minnesota made no difference. There wasn't a soul around. In Minnesota, there would have been a half-dozen jet skis buzzing around the lake and another dozen boats roaring big wakes across the glass-calm water. The lake was so pristine, the land so wild and untamed, I felt almost guilty with every step. Across the clear blue water, the deep green forest climbed for the last peaks of the Continental Divide, cut by a cascading waterfall that trickled to a slow stream before spilling into the lake. Slivers of white snow climbed down from the patchy white peaks to meet the trees. I couldn't believe there was still snow up there, in July. I could tell there was another lake feeding the waterfall. I could tell Blue wanted to go all the way. And Blue could tell I wasn't up for the challenge.

We returned the next day, Saturday, to make the upper lake. It was a whole different world. The clearing in front of the tunnel was packed with cars. The trail was packed with hikers carrying serious packs full of water, food, and gear — and dogs on leashes. By the time we made the lower lake, the water's edge was spattered with the neon colors of tents. It was no longer a wild and untamed land. The upper lake was a different story. The weekend warriors didn't dare the last steep climb to the upper lake. The water ran from dark blue in the center to crystal clear before the rusty red rock of the bed reflected through the shallows with perfect definition. Blue led me to the perfect cliff where I could hang my feet over the edge and contemplate my reflection over jerky and dry cereal.

I had no idea where Blue was leading me the following morning. We hit the river and he went the opposite direction. And when we reached the eastern line that he had trained me so well not to pass, he kept right on going. I stopped before crossing that imaginary line, and the biggest smile crossed Blue's face as if he were saying, "good boy." Then he circled back to nudge me across the line. I didn't even worry when we passed the NO TRESPASSING signs. Then a gunshot dropped me to the ground. "Yer on private property, flatlander!" a gravelly voice echoed across the gorge. I had no idea where it was coming from — I was still checking my body for holes and scurrying for the cover of a fallen tree. When I was finally sure I hadn't been hit, I peeked over the tree to see Blue charging up the ridge to my right. Ahead of him, I spotted the silhouette of a man in a cowboy hat. He was standing high above on a rock bluff, staring at me down the barrel of a rifle. He never saw Blue coming. I thought Blue was going to tear the guy apart as he sailed through the air toward the man. And then he dropped right at the man's feet and went all wiggly before rolling over on his back. The old man dropped the gun and started rubbing Blue's belly.

"Come on up and get yer dog, boy," the old man hollered.

"He's not mine."

"You sure 'bout that?"

All I could think was the crazy bastard was trying to trick me into coming out into the open — he obviously knew the dog. It was probably his, I thought. Then Blue started barking. I was certain he was trying to tell me to join him. But, by that point, I was seriously considering Blue to somehow be in cahoots with the old man and his "kill the flatlander" plan. It wasn't until Blue ran down to me and started nudging me to get up that I finally climbed out from behind the tree. By then, the man had slung his rifle over his shoulder and was walking towards me. I cautiously approached him while making sure I had cover to dive for in case he raised his rifle. The closer I got, the more nervous I became. He was an old man. His hair was stark white, as was his bushy beard. He was wearing some sort of tattered leather suit with frills hanging from under the arms like something you would expect to see an old Indian chief wearing, with a cowhide leather cowboy hat pulled down tight to shadow his weathered face.

"Clancy's the name," he said with a high-pitched drawl as he brushed his grubby hands on his dirty pants before offering me a handshake. "You must be Jack."

My jaw dropped, wondering how the hell that crazy old bastard knew my name.

"You look like you need a drink, boy," Clancy laughed as he walked away. Blue followed alongside. "You comin'?" Clancy asked, without turning around to see that I wasn't following.

"Is that your dog?"

"It's yer dog."

"He's not mine."

Clancy stopped and turned around.

"Yer Jack, ain't ya?"

"How do you know my name?"

"You got Martin's shack?"

"Yeah."

"You must be Jack."

I have no idea what made me follow that crazy old mountain man. Everything inside of me screamed RUN. But something about the way Blue trotted alongside him told me that everything would be okay. Clancy's shack was about ten minutes away. It was built right into the side of the mountain — it made Martin's shack look big and well built. Piles of scrap metal were heaped all around the clearing surrounding the shack. Weathered sheds, leaning from the years, were scattered along the perimeter and spilling over with junk. The crooked steps creaked as Clancy climbed onto his porch.

"You hungry?" Clancy asked over the sound of his squeaky front door.

"No thanks," I answered as my stomach growled. I was so hungry, but there was no way I was eating anything that grubby old mountain man made. Blue, on the other hand, was immediately sitting at full attention at the question.

"Yeah, yer always hungry, ain't ya, Blue?"
Blue's tail wagged his affirmation.

Clancy stomped around in his shack, crashing and banging, for a good five minutes before returning. I was seriously considering making a run for it. But Blue wouldn't have it. I called him and called him — by his name for the first time — but he wouldn't move. He just sat staring at the door and drooling. Suddenly the door swung open to show Clancy's crazy silhouette in the doorway. He was waving a big bloody bone in one hand and a giant jug in the other.

"WOW!" Clancy hollered and shook his head after taking a pull from the jug. "You think you want this?" he teased Blue with the bone. Blue never flinched, until Clancy said, "Okay." Blue quickly snatched the bone and scurried under the porch to chew his bone in peace.

"What kind of bone is that?" I asked, thinking it looked an awful lot like a human leg bone.

"Moose femur. Got him last week," Clancy answered as he handed me his jug.

I grabbed the jug, took a pull, and blew fire from my mouth.

"Good shit, hey boy?" Clancy laughed. "That's me great-grandpappy's recipe. He brought the recipe all the way from Mississippi when he headed west in the spring of 1857. Grandpappy Orville was only seventeen when he left home in search of gold. He found it in a river not far from here in early 1858 and staked his claim months before that phony John Gregory came along to claim himself as the first person to discover gold in the gorge that now bears his name."

I sat on that old man's porch passing his jug of homemade hooch and listening to him tell the most outrageous stories for the rest of the afternoon. He was the most interesting character I had ever met. It turns out he and Martin had been good friends since Martin settled here in the early seventies. He knew everything about the area. He told me all about the big fire of 1874 that burned all of Central City to the ground. Orville's shanty was one of the first to burn. His claim was right in the middle of what was to become Main Street. "They lost everything when the big fire roared," Clancy groaned. "Everyone lost everything. Thousands upon thousands were left to sleep out under the cover of nothing more than the stars, for months. Wasn't long after that the greed heads swooped in and ruined the town. They made everyone file papers to lay claim to the property that they had already settled on as their own long ago. And Orville had moved high into the mountains for the very reason of avoiding such oversight by the impending government in which he didn't believe. He wasn't about to pay no filing fee to some scheisty land grabber just to get a piece of paper that said he owned the property he had settled years before. And that's exactly what them government weasels wanted. They were pushing to organize the territory. They were pushing to make Colorado a state. And they laid claim to his property the moment the filing deadline was over. His plot was the perfect location for the saloon. The newly appointed sheriff kicked Orville off his claim the very next day." Clancy took a long pull off the jug. "You know what the first building permit they issued was for?"

"What?"

"The new saloon. What do you s'pose was the last permit they issued?"

"I have no idea."

"The shoe repair store," Clancy burst into a heehaw hillbilly laugh that I later learned would follow most of his stories. "It seems City Council had an eye on the spiritous needs of the citizens, rather than for their soles." Clancy's tone turned serious as if he had just shared some deep dark secret into human behavior.

Dusk was settling on the horizon behind the trees when Clancy abruptly told me to leave. The seriousness on his face told me I had done something wrong. But he was quick to inform me that it was for nothing more than my own safety. "There's a mountain lion that hunts the forest between our properties at night."

"A mountain lion?" My eyes were wide with panic.

"You'll be fine," Clancy patted me on the back, "long's you get back to yer shack before dark."

As far as I know, I encountered no mountain lion as I stumbled home. But to be honest with you, I was so drunk from Clancy's shine I don't even remember the walk. All I know is that I woke up the next morning on the floor of my shack, fully clothed and in a puddle of drool, to Clancy pounding on my door.

"What?!" I grumbled as I opened the door.

"You plannin' on spendin' the winter?"

"I don't know," I answered, knowing I had never even considered it. Even before hearing Clancy's stories, just the day before, about single snowfalls piling up to over five feet deep, I was certain I could never winter here, especially without any heat or electricity.

"Well, if you are, we got lotsa work to do."

After sucking down a gallon of water straight from the spigot, I followed Clancy into the yard. My head was pounding so badly Clancy's high-pitched chatter was scrambled. All I knew was he was wandering around the property knocking on dead trees. And I followed, nodding my aching head like I knew what he was saying, with Blue nipping at my heels for breaking our routine.

"Wood's more valuable than gold," Clancy chirped as we returned to the shack.

We spent the rest of the day felling all the dead trees around the shack that Clancy said were dry enough to burn with an old two-man handsaw. I forgot all about my hangover within an hour. We must have dropped a dozen big pines and cut them into eight-foot lengths that we then dragged to the back of the shack. Once we had hauled everything to the pile behind the shack, we cut them all into sixteen-inch sections. My hands were a blistery, bloody mess by the time we were done.

"You best get to splittin' this if you wanna get it done before the snow flies," Clancy snickered as he turned and headed home.

I headed straight to bed and fell sound asleep long before the sun set — I bet I was sawing logs before Clancy got home. It was still dark when I awoke to a rumbling stomach. As hungry as I was, I couldn't force myself to roll over, let alone climb out of bed. My whole body was sore. Had it not been for Blue pulling off my covers and then tugging at my pant leg, I wouldn't have gotten out of bed all day. But Blue was relentless, and he dragged me onto the porch to witness the best sunrise I had ever seen. The sky was consumed with such a red intensity that the whole valley smoldered in pink. I could have sat on the porch all day if not for Blue's pestering. He was not about to be screwed out of his daily adventure for two days in a row. He started by nudging my legs. I ignored him. He turned to tugging at my pant legs. I didn't budge. That's when he engaged his secret weapon — the stare. He sat as perfectly still as a statue with his head cocked just slightly to the right. You didn't even have to be looking at him to feel the intensity beaming from his eyes. But if you didn't look, squeaky whimpers were quick to follow the stare. I was following Blue into the forest before the sun had burned the pink away.

A walk in the wilderness was just what I needed. I was feeling pretty good when we got back to the shack for lunch.

"What do you think, boy?" I tossed a chunk of jerky to Blue. "Should I spend the winter?"

Blue devoured the jerky and came over and sat on my foot. At first, I thought he had only come to beg for more, until he started rubbing his ear into my hand. He wanted me to pet him. Knowing many normal dogs, I understand how this probably doesn't seem like a big deal. Every dog I had ever met before Blue was a sucker for a good rub down. I could always find that sweet spot that would send the back leg twitching. Not Blue. He didn't like to be petted, anywhere, especially the top of his head. To this day I haven't found that spot, but Blue let me scratch his ears, as much as he hated it, and I took that to mean that he wanted me to stay. I split wood the rest of that afternoon — and two hours a day, every day, for the next month.

A few days passed before Clancy returned. I was splitting wood when he snuck up on me. He waited until I was just swinging the axe to announce his presence.

"Watch yer feet!" Clancy hollered in my ear.

I completely missed the log and nearly chopped off my toes. Clancy shook with laughter.

"You gotta spread yer legs, boy," Clancy laughed.

Before I turned to face Clancy, I looked at Blue with a scowl.

"Thanks for the warning." I could tell from his smile he knew exactly what Clancy was doing. He even let out a laughing little bark to rub it in.

"That's all you got split?" Clancy pointed to my pile.

"You takin' a trip?" I gestured at the big green duffle bag hanging from his shoulder.

"Thought you could use some real clothing," Clancy said with a smirk as he looked over my shredded button-down shirt and tattered khaki pants. They were nothing more than rags after only three days of work.

Clancy led me into the shack to unload the duffle bag. It was packed full with everything from socks to sweaters. And he had instructions on how and when to wear everything.

"Weather's gonna be changin' here quicker than you think. Come September, you gotta dress for a blizzard on even the sunniest of days." Clancy said the temperature could easily drop fifty degrees in a minute when a front rolls over the Divide. "That beautiful blue sky can turn black as night, in the middle of the day, when a storm settles in the valley."

Clancy stopped by every afternoon that week with a duffle bag full of gear. He brought me bags full of tattered wool sweaters, jackets, gloves, hats, snowshoes, boots... One day he even brought over this hideous old one-piece black snowmobile suit with blazed orange stripes down the sides — the thing must have weighed twenty pounds — it filled the whole duffle bag.

"That thing'll keep you toasty at forty below," Clancy laughed.

"Don't you need this stuff?"

"Ain't mine, don't fit."

"Where'd you get it?"

"It was Martin's... you guys were about the same size."

CHAPTER 2

It must have been early August when I finally had all my wood split. Keeping track of the days was next to impossible with no phone, television, Internet, or calendar. I hadn't even been to town for weeks. All I know is that the days were already starting to get shorter and Clancy was desperately trying to teach me how to live off the land before the snow fell. His first lesson was on fishing. "A man that can't feed himself don't deserve to live," was Clancy's favorite line. We spent one whole day along the creek. I practiced casting on land while Clancy demonstrated over the creek — he insisted I master the basics before I got my fly wet. He was an absolute artist with his fly rod. He pulled a rainbow trout from the river with every cast. I spent the whole day untangling my line — and cleaning Clancy's catch. He insisted I clean every fish so that I would know how to do it when I was alone. I insisted I had it down after the second trout. Clancy disagreed — only because he didn't want to do it.

I had never had a better meal than Clancy's trout cooked over an open campfire. He cooked two over the fire for our dinner and then brought the rest home to smoke into jerky for the winter. "Store it in a cool and dry place and it will last all winter," Clancy claimed.

The second half of Clancy's living-off-the-land lesson was

hunting. I was far less than thrilled about killing a living animal than I was about cleaning a fish. I had never fired a gun in my life. Clancy's 30-30 bolt action was the first lesson. He tacked a target to a tree, we hiked back almost three hundred yards, and Clancy blasted eight rounds into the bull's-eye.

"It's all about yer breathing," Clancy instructed as he handed the rifle to me. We had already hiked back to within seventy yards of the target. I hit the edge of the target once out of nine shots — Clancy was not impressed.

We shot everything from handguns to shotguns to machine guns in the days to follow. Clancy's .9mm handgun was my favorite.

"What kind of animals you hunt with a handgun?" I asked.

"The worst kind."

It was late fall when Clancy said I was ready to take my first elk. It was a beautiful morning. The approaching sunrise had barely turned the night's sky gray as we left Clancy's shack. I was shaking like a leaf when Clancy handed me his rifle. I prayed the whole way that we wouldn't see anything. But Clancy was sure the herd would be drinking from the creek shortly after the sun climbed just over the big pine tree on the other side of the river, "That's about 8 a.m. this time of year." Apparently, elk are creatures of habit. "You can set your watch by them things," Clancy chuckled. We set up on that same rock bluff looking over the river where I first saw Clancy. I remember being so relieved when the sun had climbed higher than the big pine and no elk had come to drink. Then Clancy turned to me with a smile. I don't know if his hearing was so good that he heard them coming, maybe he could smell the stinky beasts; whatever the case, thirty seconds later the herd came snorting and rustling through the brush to the river. Four cows were first to step to the water (Clancy says the females are called cows. The males are bulls). "Watch their tails," Clancy whispered. "See how they're flickering like Morse code?" he whispered. "That's how they communicate to the bulls; the bulls always follow the cows." Then the flickering stopped. "Here he comes." Clancy put his finger to his mouth as a big bull crashed through the brush to the river. His rack hung high on his head like two giant oak trees. I looked to Clancy, expecting him to tell me to fire. He just shook his head, never taking his eyes off the river. Moments later, an old gray bull stumbled to the river. He was much smaller than the first bull, but he was the one Clancy wanted me to take. Clancy said it was his time. The big bull had another three or four good years of fathering young. The old boy wouldn't make it through the winter. "If you only kill the trophies, ain't gonna be no trophies left," he said. It made sense. It sounded responsible. So, I took a deep breath, held it in, and slowly pulled the trigger just like Clancy had taught me. And I hit that old bull right behind the shoulder just like I was supposed to. The old bull dropped like a sack of potatoes. I felt horrible. And I had to sit there, still, pondering the murder of that poor majestic animal from high above on that rocky bluff for another twenty minutes before we could move. Clancy said we had to let it bleed out; otherwise we'd spook it and have to track it all day.

Clancy was quick to recognize the anguish in my eyes. He assured me the old elk would have fallen sick this winter and been picked apart by coyotes while he was still alive. I was just about to let myself feel better about my murderous actions when we approached the steaming body.

"This was Martin's," Clancy said as he presented me a knife. "You should have it. Never leave home without it." The thing was huge. The blade alone was eight inches long, with a roaring lion etched into one side of the blade. The silver handle, inlaid with ivory, narrowed to the head of an eagle at the butt. The flip side of the blade was etched with a Spanish inscription: *No es el leon como lo pintan a lo major es mas feo*. "The Lion is not always as it is pictured, it may be worse," was burned into the handmade leather sheath. It was such a thing of beauty, I didn't want to soil it with blood. Clancy assured me it had seen its fair share. So, I followed Clancy's instruction and split that poor beast from his privates to his neck. His guts alone weighed more than me. And just as I rolled that steaming pile of intestines onto the ground, Clancy was hacking the old beast into pieces with a bone saw.

There wasn't a second to spare on small talk. Clancy said we had less than an hour to get the entire kill back to his shack before the flies settled in. But I got the feeling there was also a legal reason for hauling that big beast away before anyone noticed. Clancy had a big open backpack that he would load full of meat and make me carry back to his shack, a hundred pounds at a time. Even Blue had his own saddlebag contraption that could carry a good fifty pounds at a time. It took us six heavy trips before we had the beast back at Clancy's shack.

"Never take an animal you can't preserve," was the one point Clancy really tried to drive home. With no electricity or refrigeration, we had precious little time. The afternoon sun was fast approaching. The temperature was already pushing sixty — unseasonably warm for the time of year, according to Clancy. Anything that wasn't in Clancy's "cooler" within two hours of the kill would be spoiled. Clancy's "cooler" was an abandoned mineshaft cut into the mountainside behind his shack. The shaft dropped a good twenty feet underground before opening into a cavern. It was at least thirty degrees cooler down there. I had to wear one of Clancy's old flannels to bear the cold. In the furthest corner, Clancy had constructed a ten-by-ten box out of a roll of stainless steel that "fell off the train." He had a six-foot cutting table set up inside. "Even on the hottest summer days, it never gets above forty down here."

We had that whole beast cut up and into Clancy's cooler with fifteen minutes to spare. Slicing the big chunks into strips, about a quarter-inch thick, was the next step. That was Clancy's job. My job was to take the strips and hang them in Clancy's smoker. He built a giant smoker next to his shack using an eight-foot-round steel culvert. It must have been ten feet long. He said it was left over from when they rerouted the river to flow under the bridge on the road to the train tunnel. It was from the same chunk that made Martin's roof, he said. He and Martin welded one of the leftover flattened chunks to one end of the smoker to seal it off and another to the other end, on hinges, to make a sealable door. "It took us one whole summer to reroof Martin's shack and build that damn smoker," he said, as he carved the hindquarters into strips.

Anything we couldn't get into the smoker before nightfall would be lost. And any meat wasted was a slap in the face to whatever strange God that governed Clancy's land. That was Clancy's number one rule: Never waste anything given by the almighty Mother Nature. Clancy didn't believe in God, in Biblical terms, but he was certain there was something out there responsible for creating this mountain paradise he had come to call home. He was certain he would someday be rewarded for never taking more than he needed. But more than that, he was proud of that fact. He wore it like a badge of honor. His favorite meal was rabbit, but he never took more than ten a year. "The rabbits would thrive even if I took thirty, the way they multiply," he chuckled. "But the chain above," he always got serious by this point, "the fox, the coyotes, even that bastard mountain lion would suffer if I took more than ten."

The mountain lion was Clancy's number-one enemy. The mountain lion killed King. King was Blue's brother. "I never even wanted that damn dog." Clancy always got angry shortly into his King stories. "That damn Martin had to go and talk me into getting the mutt." He would never admit it, but it was obvious that Clancy loved King. They were as inseparable as Martin and Blue. King was only two when the mountain lion took him. They were walking home from an evening at Martin's. Clancy knew better than to walk home through the woods after dark, but that night, after he and Martin polished off a whole bottle of his homemade hooch, Clancy broke his own rule. He was almost to his front door when the mountain lion pounced. It went straight for Clancy's throat. Had King not lunged at the lion's back, Clancy would've never been seen again. "Damn dog put up a hell of a fight... almost took that cat bastard, for a minute, but as thick as that stubborn mutt's skin, it was no match for the cat's razor-sharp claws." Clancy has hunted that mountain lion ever since.

And I understood. A few days with Blue, and I knew. My family always had dogs when I was growing up; they were all good dogs, but they were all pets. Blue was more like a person than a dog. He understood almost every word I said. He definitely knew all the swear words. Even something as silly as me letting out a "Dammit!" after stubbing my toe on the log bedpost was enough to send Blue racing for the doggie door — I had to run for bed after blowing out the lantern to make it before the darkness engulfed the shack. Clancy said Martin had a bit of a temper and Blue always knew to "skedaddle" as soon as the first "shit!" was sworn. He said Martin worked on training Blue, every single day, for the first two years. He could make Blue do anything he wanted him to do with different whistles. Martin could get Blue to stop on a dime — even while chasing a rabbit — and immediately run back to sit at his side. "The inside-out whistle, Martin called it." Clancy shook his head with a grin as he let out a shrieking whistle. "You suck the air in rather than blow," he chuckled as Blue bolted in through the doggie door. Poor Blue looked so sad. I think it was the first time he had heard the inside-out whistle since Martin died. Clancy said Blue was devastated when it happened. He said Martin died watching the sunset. His favorite thing was to smoke a joint and watch the sunset and sunrise from the porch. He sat frozen, in early April, for three days before Clancy found him. Blue never left his side. It wasn't until Blue passed out from hunger and exhaustion that Clancy was able to pry Martin's frozen body from his seat. He hadn't seen Blue again, until the day we met.

With that big elk hanging in the smoker, Clancy started a fire in the fire pit between the smoker and his shack.

"You gettin' hungry, boy?"

"Starving."

Clancy grabbed a bottle of his homemade hooch off the wire-spool table next to the pit, took a pull, and then tossed the bottle to me.

"I think I'll pass on the liquid dinner."

"That's just the appetizer," Clancy laughed as he held up two giant steaks. "Never smoke the backstraps."

Blue was instantly Clancy's best friend.

"Ain't no chance in hell yer gettin' any of this, dog." Clancy turned his back to Blue as he dropped the steaks into an old cast-iron skillet. Blue's whimpering stare had no effect on Clancy.

"Pass me back that bottle, boy"

I walked over and handed the bottle to Clancy. He took a quick pull and then splashed the steaks with a shot of whiskey.

"Whiskey on the steaks?"

"That's how you get the spices to stick." Clancy grabbed a small brown paper bag off the table, grabbed a handful of pine needles out of it, and dropped them into an old tin gold pan.

"You're not seriously going to put pine needles on the steaks?" I asked as Clancy ground the dried needles into dust.

"Pine needles and reindeer moss." Clancy grabbed another bag off the table, grabbed a handful of light green moss, and ground it in with the needles.

I thought he was just messing with me until he dropped the two steaks into the mix, made sure they were completely covered, threw them back in the pan, and put the pan over the fire.

I was skeptical, to say the least. Had the steaks not smelled so good, I might not have dared try Clancy's special seasoning. But I did. And it was the best steak I had ever eaten. The reason might have had more to do with the pride of providing for oneself than the seasoning. Whatever the case, they were damn good steaks. Even Blue got to feast on a big bowl of raw trimmings Clancy served him right after he delivered my sizzling steak.

With our plates licked clean, we pulled our chairs to face the fire. The sun had just passed the tree line to the west and the cold mountain air was settling in.

"I 'er tell you 'bout the time I killed a giant muntjac?" Clancy passed me the bottle.

I grabbed the bottle and took a pull; I figured I better be a little drunk if Clancy was going to start in with the tall tales — he was already pretty well ripped by that point.

"What's a giant muntjac?" I asked, expecting Clancy to describe some cyclops-like bigfoot creature — just a few hours earlier he was trying to convince me he trapped jackalopes in the winter by setting trip lines just high enough to snare their antlers as they hop down the trail.

"Muntjac's are funny-looking red deer with angry black faces and straight-back horns like the devil."

"Red deer?"

"In 'Nam. We'd been eatin' nothin' but bugs for days. Private Nelson from Arkansas and me were the only ones left. The radio'd been shot to shit with the rest of 'em days before. Rations were long gone. That's when the muntjac scurried past our hole. We knew the shot would attract Charlie, but Nelson and I were both too hungry to care. Best damn steak I 'er ate."

Apparently, Clancy voluntarily enlisted for Vietnam. He said his father never spoke to him again. They quickly realized he was a skilled marksman and Clancy was trained as a sniper. He re-enlisted twice before he had had enough. He was barely back in the States when JFK was assassinated.

"You know that was the work of the CIA?" Clancy slurred.

"I thought it was the FBI?" I joked.

"Them FBI bozos couldn't put something like that together."

"How do you know it was the CIA?"

"There's a shit-ton of evidence, but the most obvious was the third shot. It was definitely a .308 exploding round. CIA was the only one with such ballistic technology back then."

"Why would they want to kill him?"

"Kennedy scared the shit out of the intelligence community. Not only did he disregard most of their intelligence as propaganda, but he was an uncontrollable maverick set on dismantling all that Hoover had created for them. But it was his hankering for the fairer sex that aroused his demise. Things were heating up between the U.S. and Russia after the commies delivered nukes to Cuba. The entire intelligence community was urging Kennedy to nuke the commies. But Kennedy refused. Not only did he refuse, but he would sneak Marilyn Monroe into the White House for evenings of watching the radar for nukes while eating acid and snorting blow."

"Kennedy ate acid in the White House?"

"Among other things," Clancy cackled. "That was all the

CIA needed to consider Kennedy a threat to national security and begin to plot his assassination. Took them spook bastards over a year to plan the president's execution. Only took 'em a few days to kill Marilyn with a sleeping pill enema."

Clancy slurred his way right into his next tale before I had a chance to call bullshit.

"You 'er hear of a band called The Doors?"

"Yeah, Jim Morrison…"

"Exactly, Jim Morrison," Clancy cut me off. "A troubled young man, that one was."

"You knew Jim Morrison?"

"Met him in August 1966…" Clancy tossed a log on the fire and paused to watch the sparks flicker and dance into the dark night sky like stars burning to dust. "I was living out of my duffle bag, wandering up and down the California coast, camping on the beaches. I had just finished my nightly dinner of a can of beans cooked over a campfire on Hollywood Beach when Summer strolled along with a jug of wine. She was a golden-haired beauty. Nearly tripped over my fire before she saw it. 'What are you doing down there?' she asked me, once she finally noticed me lying in the sand next to the fire. Lookin' at the stars, I told her as I pointed to the hazy blue sky. 'I don't see no stars,' she said as she dove into the sand at my side. You want me to show you the Big Dipper? I winked. She reached right for my pecker and said, 'I want you to do more than show it to me.' She knew what I was talkin' 'bout. Normally you gotta look down at yer crotch before they get it. Sometimes you gotta grab it."

"Bullshit," I interrupted.

"What?"

"You want me to believe that you asked a girl if you could show her your 'Big Dipper' and she slept with you?"

"The Big Dipper, I asked her if she wanted to see *the* Big Dipper… And I wouldn't say she slept with me — that gone girl screwed me till I saw cartoons. The tab of acid she fed me may have had something to do with that. We musta went a dozen dirty rounds, rollin' in the sand. You ever had sex on the beach?"

"Can't say that I have."

"You ain't missed out. It's a rough and gritty experience. Nearly scraped all the skin off my pecker. I was pickin' sand out of my crack fer a week." Clancy trailed off into silence and stared into the fire.

"Good story, I especially like the part about Jim Morrison," I replied after a few moments of Clancy's silence.

"Jim Morrison?"

"He was a troubled young man…"

"Oh, shit, yeah, Jim Morrison. I saw him at Whiskey a Go Go. That Summer drug me there after she had her way with me on the beach. Then she disappeared into the crowd of stinky hippies. Soon's she left my side, the whole damn crowd turned into cartoon cavemen. Almost made it out the door, till the rattlesnake rhythm of the band caught my attention. The cartoon-caveman crowd was writhin' like the sea. And that Morrison was moaning 'bout riding snakes. Between his hypnotic voice and Summer's acid, the next thing I know, I'm riding some ancient snake through the crowd. Longest song I ever heard. It just kept goin' and goin'. Then that crazy Morrison started singing 'bout screwin' his mother. Got his ass dragged right off the stage. The crowd went berserk. Barely got outta there with my life." Clancy threw a log on the fire.

"So, you didn't really meet him?"

"Meet who?"

"Jim Morrison."

"Hell yeah, I met him. I was just gettin' to that," Clancy sat back. "Met him as I was walkin' back to the beach, 'bout a block from the club. Crazy bastard stepped outta the shadows to ask me if he could bum a smoke. Scared the shit outta me. Damn near stabbed the dumb bastard. Told him I didn't smoke and kept walkin'. And he started following me. Followed two steps behind me fer a whole block. When I finally pulled my knife, and told him if he kept following me I would slit his throat, all he did was ask if I was in the war. I turned around and started walking away, and the crazy fool kept following me, pestering me with questions about the war. 'You ever kill anyone?' was the question he asked me just as we reached the beach. Eighty-seven men, I said as I sprung around and jammed my knife tight to his throat. You wanna be number eighty-eight? I asked him, as I pressed the blade harder to his throat. The boy never even flinched. That's when I realized it was Morrison. I dropped my knife and led him to my fire. Then he rambled on and on about conjuring spirits. Told me he conjured the spirits of dark angels before he hit the stage every night to guide him through the show. Then Summer stumbled back fer another dirty round and that Morrison bastard stole her away. I had my thumb in the air for Lost Creek the very next morning."

The sun had long set and the fire was dying when Clancy finished his Doors story. I was in no shape to walk back to my shack — even if Clancy would have let me. I was sprawled out across his floor to hear one more tale before I was out cold. It was some story about the Caribou Ranch, some recording studio outside of Nederland where Clancy said every musician from Prince to Peter Frampton had recorded. I was in and out of consciousness by that time, but from what I remember Clancy wanted me to believe that he worked at the Caribou Ranch recording studio after he returned to Lost Creek. He claimed he met every famous musician of the times from Elton John to John Lennon. "You know that song 'Rock and Roll, Hoochie Koo' by Rick Derringer?"

I nodded. The last thing I remember is Clancy telling me how he helped Joe Walsh with the guitar riff.

We spent the following week at Crater Lake. Clancy was bound and determined to teach me how to survive in the wild. He taught me what to look for when setting up the tent. He pointed out all the edible plants, as well as the poisonous ones to stay away from. He taught me how to build a proper fire pit to prevent forest fires — it was an extremely dry summer. The trail was littered with NO CAMPFIRES signs all the way up. "That's fer the flatlanders," Clancy said. The key to building a proper fire pit, according to Clancy, was to find the biggest rock you can roll out of the ground and unearth it. Around the hole left from the rock, you stacked flat rocks about two feet high, slowly funneling narrower towards the top. "Always keep the fire small enough so that the flames can't flicker over the rim." Clancy even packed a roll of metal mesh to drape over the rim to keep any sparks from flying away. "Every little spark has the potential to torch thousands of acres," Clancy warned. "Pile a few rocks on top the mesh and you can cook your meals right on the screen." We cooked fresh trout from Crater Lake for lunch and dinner every day that week.

"Always carry a lighter," Clancy chuckled as he sparked the fire with his Zippo on the last night.

"You had that the whole time!?" He had made me rub sticks until my palms were blistered every night prior.

"Had to make sure you could do without," Clancy laughed.

I learned many valuable lessons that week. "Never drink the water, no matter how clean and clear it looks," was the one rule Clancy really tried to assert. "Dehydration kicks in fast when you're pissin' out yer ass. If you gotta drink it, boil it. You ain't never gonna get rid of the chemical contaminants leftover from the mining days, but at least you'll kill the bacteria — that's what gets ya."

As much as I learned about surviving in the great outdoors, it paled in comparison to what I learned about the life of Martin. Clancy told me all about how Jack London was Martin's hero. He said Martin loved his writing, but it was London's adventurous life that he really admired. I learned Crater Lake was Martin's favorite place in the world as Clancy flipped the trout that very first night. The next day, Clancy took me to a tree at the edge of the lake.

"This is the very spot I cremated the best friend I've ever known. He always told me he wanted his ashes spread in Crater Lake. You better tell someone much younger than me, I always answered. Had to carry his frozen body all the way up the trail. You shoulda seen the looks I got from the snowshoers I passed," Clancy laughed. "Took all morning to gather enough wood for the fire. Took all afternoon to carve that damn inscription." Clancy pointed to the tree. It was a creepy old red pine whose crooked branches reached long shadows over the water. The dark red bark was thick and heavy, except for a patch at eye level that was carved to the white wood. It was roughly the size of a sheet of paper.

"Screw the hill, I climbed the mountain. Nothing left, I can't come down," I read the inscription on the tree aloud.

"Martin wrote that," Clancy informed. "Said if he was ever so unlucky as to get stuck in a regular man's grave, that's what he wanted on his tombstone. I figured the least I could do was carve it into the tree."

Clancy brought a big jug of his homemade hooch and would get pretty nostalgic after a few pulls around the campfire. He first met Martin by chance when he picked him up hitchhiking along Peak to Peak Highway. They hit it off immediately. Clancy had just returned from his post-war travels. He had just bought his property along Lost Creek. Martin was nineteen and lost, wandering the country, dodging the law after dodging the draft. "He was smart enough to steer clear of that bullshit war — that's what I first liked about him," Clancy snorted as he passed me the bottle. Martin was on his way to Canada when Clancy convinced him to spend the summer in Lost Creek. He said Martin was in love after the first month. They lived together in Clancy's shack for almost four years, panning for gold, before Martin was able to save enough money to purchase the property adjoining Clancy's. Winter was Martin's favorite season. He loved to ski. He would hike down to the train tracks every morning in the winter and hop the coal train just before it sped up out of Lost Creek. The train would get him through the tunnel where he could jump off just in time to catch the first chair at Winter Park. He skied every day the resort was open. The five o'clock zipper was timed perfectly to bring him back to Lost Creek after the lifts closed.

I felt like I knew everything about Martin after that week at Crater Lake. It never registered, at the time, why Clancy was filling me so full of the tales of Martin. I just thought he was trying to keep the memory of his good friend alive.

It was our last night at Crater Lake that this tale turned into a thriller. The fire had dulled to glowing embers when Clancy leaned toward the fiery orange glow. His leathery face turned stone serious.

"Can I trust you?"

"Yeah."

Clancy leaned back to survey our surroundings like there might be someone lurking in the darkness. When he was sure no one was close enough to listen, he returned his face to the fire's glow.

"Martin was murdered."

"What?"

"He was poisoned."

"By who?"

"Darla Campbell."

According to Clancy, there was a family of serial killers living in Lost Creek — the Campbells. "They've been killing off outsiders fer a hundred years. The head of the family is Sheriff Campbell. He's been killing under the shield of his badge since he was first elected back in 1964. His daughter, Darla, is the drug-dealing bartender at the Wagon Wheel Saloon."

"I suppose it all started when Martin met Travis," Clancy continued. "Travis was a crude little bastard, musta been in his twenties when Martin took him in. Blue was just a pup. But that didn't stop him from chasing Travis into an alley for trying to steal a case of beer out of the back of Martin's truck. Travis was hitchhiking west, running from something back East. I told Martin he should have nothing to do with him. But of course, he didn't listen. No, that Martin thought it would be a good idea to move Travis into Lost Creek. They lived together in Martin's shack for almost two years before they started building Travis his own shack. They had cut down all the trees the summer before."

"Down by the river?" I asked. I knew exactly where he was talking about; I came across the spot on the second or third day of Blue's property tour — the shack was a pile of charred logs.

"That's the spot. They worked all day, every day, that spring. Finished it in early June. They were supposed to set out on Martin's annual hike across Colorado on the Colorado Trail a few weeks later, but that dumbass Travis had to go and run his mouth at the Wagon Wheel. Dumb bastard never could hold his alcohol. He just had to go on and on about how he had built a new shack in Lost Creek and how he was now a local. Travis burned to death in his new bunk that very night. The police report claimed the fire was started after the victim fell asleep with a lit cigarette. The kid had a lot of bad habits, but smoking wasn't one. The ruble reeked of gasoline, but Sheriff Campbell wouldn't hear of it. That sonofabitch told Martin he was gonna ticket him for erecting a permanent dwelling without a permit if he pushed the issue. The sheriff's insistence alone was enough to pique Martin's suspicions. He spent the better part of the next two years investigating Sheriff Campbell. I told him to leave it alone..." Clancy took a pull, "stubborn sonofabitch. He just couldn't let it be. Just had to keep digging. He was certain Sheriff Campbell was responsible for the deaths of at least ten other people. But he never even considered that the whole family was a bunch of psychopaths. He never saw it coming. He only bought pot from Darla to get close to her father. He never once suspected her to be a killer. Hell, I would have never suspected her had I not found that joint frozen between Martin's fingers."

During the entire story, Clancy's face never read anything but dead serious. Most stories, I would catch a slight smirk or a devious look to the left and I would know, at the very least, he was embellishing a good bit. But everything he said was with deadpan, gray eyes.

"Will you help me?" Clancy's eyes were as helpless as a toddler's.

"Of course," I agreed, only because I thought it would be exciting, not because I actually believed him. I had no idea what I was getting myself into.

CHAPTER 3

We packed up camp early the following morning and hiked down the mountain in complete silence as the sun burned golden on the dark green pines. We shared a nod when we reached Clancy's shack and Blue and I continued on down the trail for home. You can't imagine how wonderful that old straw mattress felt after a week of sleeping on a rock. I slept late into the following morning.

I was startled out of bed early the following morning by Clancy banging on my door.

"Big day, my boy." Clancy rushed in with the clanging of tin to shake me out of bed faster than any alarm. "Time to learn how to earn a buck off the mountain." His old tattered canvas pack was strapped with buckets and gold pans.

"What are you talking about?"

"You said you'd help."

An hour later we were sifting sand on the shore of a hidden stream that spills into Lost Creek just past Clancy's shack.

"Whenever you need money, just ask the river for a bit of her precious yellow metal."

"What do we need money for?"

"Pot."

"Pot?"

Clancy's big plan was to have me get close to Darla so she would sell me pot, and then piss her off enough so she wanted to kill me.

"You want me to piss off a serial killer!?" I cried.

"Exactly."

"What happens if I get her to sell to me?"

"I have a professor friend in Boulder that will test it for toxins."

I was certain Clancy was full of shit. I was certain he was just trying to teach me some elaborate life lesson. But the thrill of pretending to be some sort of private investigator on the trail of a psychopathic serial killer quickly clouded my judgment. The next thing I knew, Clancy was pointing to a shiny nugget washing clear on my screen as I poured water over the box of sand Clancy had just filled.

"You found a good one there, boy." Clancy pointed as I pulled a gold nugget the size of a marble out of the box. I was sure Clancy was messing with me and slipped in a piece of fool's gold when I wasn't looking.

We drove down the hill to Black Hawk that afternoon to the only place to ever exchange your gold, according to Clancy. He made me take the nugget to the counter. I was sure the old-timer behind the counter was going to laugh me out of the joint when I handed him the nugget. Instead, his eyes lit up and he asked if he could take it into the backroom to examine it further. I looked to Clancy to see him nod. I agreed. The old man waddled back ten minutes later and offered five hundred bucks for that little yellow rock.

"Six," Clancy grumbled.

"Six it is," the old-timer howled before flipping six crisp hundred-dollar bills on the counter.

"Coulda got seven outta him with today's prices, but we ain't got time to dicker."

I met Darla the very next day. It was lunchtime at the Wagon Wheel. Built in 1868, according to the sign on the red barn exterior, the massive barn was originally the Toll Gate Barn for the Butterfield Stage Coach Company. The interior was all wood, decorated with strange art like a deer head made entirely from old cowboy boots that hung over the bar. My mission, for that first day, was to have a couple beers over lunch and try to make friends with Darla and the locals. I was not, under any circumstances, to try to buy pot from Darla. There was nothing for Clancy to worry about. I couldn't even talk to her. She was so sexy, a petite little blonde with perfect curves. But it was her eyes that got me, those crystal blue eyes that seem to burn both innocent and naughty. At first, I thought there was no way she was the Darla that Clancy had told me about. He said she was in her early forties. I would've sworn she was in her late twenties. I was barely able to spit out my order when she leaned over the bar and turned those eyes on me.

"A bacon cheeseburger and a Mich Golden Light, please," I sputtered.

"What the hell's a Mich Golden Light?"

"It's beer," I whimpered.

"We don't sell none of that piss beer here," Darla scolded. She was even sexier when she got angry. "Think you can handle an IPA?"

"What's an IPA?"

"It's real beer."

"Sounds good."

Darla rolled her eyes, poured me an IPA, and skipped back to the kitchen.

There were two old mountain men bellied up to the dark mahogany bar when I sat down. A third stumbled in while Darla was still in the kitchen. Not one of them said a single word the whole time I was there. They didn't even speak to order their drinks; they just pointed to their empty glasses and Darla would skip over and fill them. My first mission to the Wagon Wheel was a complete failure.

I had lunch at the Wagon Wheel every day for the next two weeks. But I couldn't work up the nerve to say anything more to Darla than my order. It wasn't until Cody Harrington, a local author, stumbled in one day and sat next to me at the bar that anyone would speak to me. Cody was like no one I had ever met.

I would say he was in his fifties, maybe sixties. Everything about him screamed hillbilly: his floppy leather cowboy hat, his scraggly beard, the big knife hanging from an old leather belt. I was certain he had somehow traveled through time to peddle moonshine to Darla. Then he started talking to me. I was immediately taken aback. I'm not sure whether it was the fact that one of those old mountain men was actually talking to me, or the strange way in which he spoke that shocked me. He had an almost East Coast accent, hidden under a southern drawl, but his speech had a certain eloquent flow.

"What brings such a fine young gentleman into a joint like this?" Cody asked just as Darla slid a pint in front of him. It didn't even register that he was talking to me. And when it finally did, I immediately looked up at Darla. I don't know whether it was my subconscious giving me away or if I was just worried what I might say in front of her, but Cody read it as I was there because I had eyes for Darla.

"Food," I finally replied. But Cody was already rolling with the jolly laughter of a fat man. Even his laughter was spectacular. He held nothing back.

"Food, yeah, I come for the 'food,' too." Cody nudged me with his elbow as he took a pull from his beer. "I'm just bustin' yer balls, kid."

Cody busted my balls for a good hour. But he did it in such a way that it was strangely enjoyable. And not just for me, the whole bar was entertained. Then he took his pint and wandered down the bar.

"Well, what a surprise, Walt's here." Cody accosted the next man down the line. I had seen Walt every day prior. He came in at the same time every day — just before Darla would bring me my lunch. He would slowly sip two brandies and then leave without saying a word. Walt was a sturdy old man — at least eighty. His hair was long, silky-white, and fell straight down to the middle of his back. He wore business-style slacks and button-up light blue dress shirts that I was certain he'd been wearing since the sixties. "You ever get yer pickup off Gypsy Mountain?" Cody patted Walt on the back as he turned to me.

The whole bar roared. "This dumb bastard got so drunk two winters ago he tried to off-road over Gypsy Mountain in a blizzard. He got stuck and had to walk... What was it, Walt, ten miles? ... He stumbled ten miles home, in a blizzard, passed out, and forgot where he got stuck. Took him all summer to find the thing. And it was all shot to shit with bullet holes when he finally did." Cody was practically rolling on the floor by the time he finished his story. Even I felt comfortable enough to laugh.

"Careful, kid," Walt turned to me. "He'll be trying to sell you his book any minute now." The whole bar laughed.

"What are you laughing at, Gene?" Cody turned to the next man in line. "How's the car collection? Gene here, our local 'master carpenter' built himself a big ole garage for his classic car collection that collapsed under the first four-inch snowfall last winter."

"Why don't you tell the kid how you crapped your pants at the superbowl party last year?" Gene fired back.

"Oh! That was Darla's cooking that did that to me," Cody was quick to explain.

"Screw you, Cody," Darla countered.

"I knew you'd come around."

"In your dreams."

"Ain't that the truth?"

The whole bar was rolling until a dread-headed hippie strolled in. "Jerry!" Cody cheered. I had seen Jerry wander through and grab a beer from behind the bar or food from the kitchen a few times in the days prior. He wore the same outfit everyday: camouflage cargo shorts, a tie-dyed T-shirt, and the same silly flip-flops. I was told he was Darla's cousin. "Can't wait to hear the new album, bro!" Cody continued.

"Gettin' close, man," Jerry raised the PBR he grabbed from behind the bar and flip-flopped out the back door. The whole bar roared as soon as the door slammed. Apparently, Jerry had been working on some "top-secret, experimental, folk-funk, rock" album for the last ten years. It was obvious that no one liked Jerry, but no one wanted Jerry to know.

I must have had five or six beers before I realized I had better leave. Two had been my limit, up to that point. I was long past the stage of being able to hold my tongue. And that's when Cody pounced.

"You've been a good sport, kid," Cody patted me on the back. "Let me buy you one last final final."

"Okay." I was too ripped to refuse. I don't even remember leaving the Wagon Wheel, let alone driving home.

I was a bit nervous as I walked into the Wagon Wheel the next day, not sure what I had let slip while I was ripped.

"Jack!" Gene cheered when I walked in, "How's it hangin'?"

"Good, Gene. How are you?"

"Be a hell of a lot better if Darla'd let me show her a good time."

"You wish," Darla snarled.

"You don't know what you're missing," Gene hollered as he walked out.

"Cheeseburger, fries, and an IPA?" Darla asked me with a smile. It was the first time she remembered my order — or the first time she acknowledged it, anyway. And I smiled from ear to ear and nodded like an idiot.

"How you like livin' in Lost Creek?" Darla returned with my beer. Her question took me by surprise. I didn't remember telling anyone I lived in Lost Creek.

"Good, good, yeah I like it," I answered like a fourth grader talking to a girl under the monkey bars.

"What's that accent… where you from?"

"Minnesota."

"Minnesooota, 'Yah,' that's cute," she giggled, poking fun at my accent before trotting back to the kitchen to throw my burger on the grill.

I was jittery as a schoolboy awaiting her return. I didn't even notice Walt had slid in and sat on the stool next to me.

"You stayin' in Martin's old shack, huh?"

"Yup."

"How you know Martin?"

"I didn't."

"How you get his plot?"

"He left it to me."

"Why?"

"I honestly don't know. Clancy says Martin picked my name out of the phone book." Everyone stopped whatever they were doing and turned to face me.

"You know Clancy?" I could tell by Walt's tone, as well as the expressions staring back at me, that no one liked Clancy.

"Not really," I replied. "He shot at me one day for stepping onto his property."

"Crazy ole bastard, that Clancy. Never once left the county, but he'll tell you tales about his travels around the world."

"Remember his story about almost dying from encephalitis from a mosquito bite?" Gene chuckled.

"Oh yeah, he was saved by medicine cooked up by the daughter of Sitting Bull?" Walt answered. Everyone laughed. I tried to laugh, but it was very unconvincing due to the thoughts that Clancy had played me for a complete fool swirling around my head.

Walt had three bumps that day, instead of his normal two. I think he was staying longer than usual for the same reason I was — we were waiting to see if Cody would make another appearance. He did not.

"We won't see Cody for another month," Darla told me when I finally paid my tab.

"Cody?" I pretended not to know what she was talking about.

Walt was out the door a second later. He was the last of the "Afternooners" to leave. As soon as the door slammed behind him, Darla rushed over and locked it.

"You smoke?" Darla smiled. She didn't even wait for me to respond before trotting off through the swinging kitchen doors, giving me one last look with her crystal-blue eyes before the door swung back. I thought she was talking about cigarettes at the time, and my few experiences with smoking cigarettes were less than enjoyable, but, for some strange reason, I followed.

I found Darla smoking a joint at the grill and blowing the smoke into the hood.

"I can't handle prepping for the dinner rush without a few puffs," she said as she handed the joint to me. I took it without a single thought passing through my clouded mind. And I nearly hacked my lungs out after the first hit.

"Easy, cowboy," Darla giggled.

It was obvious it was my first time. And the four beers I had over lunch did not agree with the THC. The kitchen was spinning by the time I coughed up my third hit.

"I gotta go let my dog out," I stuttered as I stumbled for the door. I thought I was going to puke as I climbed into my car. It didn't even dawn on me that I hadn't paid my tab until I was rumbling up my driveway. My throat was so dry. My eyes itched. I puked on the front step. That's when the paranoia settled in. How could I be so stupid, I thought as the shack spun so fast I couldn't grasp the door knob. I had pretty much convinced myself that Darla had poisoned me as I collapsed into the same chair on the porch where Martin had died. And I was certain of it when a big black crow swooped down onto the railing and started talking.

"Feed me, shit bag," the crow screeched. "Where's the beef?"

I ran screaming like a little girl.

I was still screaming as I crested the last hill before Clancy's shack. Clancy was ready to gun me down as I approached his porch. He had his sights right on me. And I ran right past him and into his shack with Blue yipping at my heels. I think Clancy thought a whole Campbell clan was chasing me.

"What in tarnation's gotten into you, boy?" Clancy finally followed me in.

"I'm dyin', Clancy," I cried. "I couldn't resist her."

"What the hell you talkin' about?"

"I smoked her drugs."

"What!?"

That's about the last thing I remember about that afternoon. I woke up the next morning in Clancy's bed. Clancy was not happy with me. He chewed my ass for a good hour for being so careless and stupid. The only thing that made him smile in the slightest was when he made fun of me for freaking out about the talking crow. Apparently, I wasn't tripping. Martin had trained "Percy" the crow to say over 200 words. "That crazy old crow must be twenty years old."

I avoided the Wagon Wheel for the next few days. I can't honestly tell you why. Clancy was sure it was fear. And that's the only reason he stopped pushing me to buy pot from Darla. I'm afraid it was more along the lines of embarrassment, for many reasons. I was embarrassed about running out on my tab. I was embarrassed about not being able to handle my pot. But most of all, I was embarrassed for falling so hard for Clancy's story that I actually thought I was dying.

I was running out of excuses when a letter was delivered to my door to suppress Clancy's pressure, for a couple of days, anyway. Clancy had been stopping by in the late afternoon to check up on me — to see if I had been back to the Wagon Wheel.

"Come in!" I cried after a knock at my door. I thought it was Clancy. But the knocking continued. And for some strange reason I was afraid to answer the door. That's when Blue went nuts. We had gotten back from a hike about an hour earlier. Blue always napped in the shade behind the shack after our hikes. Blue's shrill barks were quickly followed by a scream. The door slammed open and then shut just as fast. A wide-eyed deliveryman stood panting against the door. His eyes were just fading into relief, thinking that vicious dog was stuck on the other side of the door, when Blue bolted through the doggy door — right between that poor guy's legs. His screech rattled the window. And Blue sat vigilantly at the guy's feet, staring straight into that poor guy's eyes.

"Blue, leave 'm alone," I ordered.
Blue didn't flinch.

"I need a signature," the deliveryman whined.

"Who you lookin' for?"

"Jack Leery."

"That's me." I signed for the envelope and then held Blue, so the poor guy could back out the door and run to his truck.

I tore open the envelope to be reminded I hadn't paid my student loans for quite some time. Clancy busted through the door just as I was about to toss it in the stove.

"What was that all about?"

"Just some B.S. about not paying my student loans."

"Student loans... them's federal, right, from the government?"

"Yeah."

"You best take care of them."

"I can't."

"Why."

"I owe like thirty grand."

"Thirty grand! For school? You know the library's free?" Clancy about tipped over from the thought of spending thirty grand for school. I decided not to tell him I had already paid off about twenty. He went on to tell me how I did not want to mess with the federal government when it came to money. "They're some savage bastards. 'For the people' don't apply when you owe 'em money."

We settled on hitting the river for the answer — and dinner. I hadn't been fishing with Clancy since the first time he had taken me — but I had been practicing. At first, the draw was being able to pull a free meal out of the river in my own back yard — and break the monotony of jerky and dry cereal. Not to mention the fact that I have never eaten a better meal. A little salt and pepper and trout is the tastiest meat there is — and cleaning them is easy. All you have to do is slice them up the belly and pull out their guts — it's much simpler than filleting crappies like Pops tried to teach me. But after my first solo, it was more about the art of the cast. I would spend hours practicing my "S" cast, as Clancy called it, never letting my fly lie long enough to get snatched. I could only eat one — and save none. So, I tried to perfect my aim for at least an hour, every time, before I would feed it to the fishes. I could tell Clancy noticed — even though he didn't say anything. I would catch him watching me cast, and then really float his fly, whipping and snapping, to lie just upstream from a hole he somehow knew a lunker was lurking. His line flowed effortlessly. His fly dropped true. And he snagged one with every cast. "You gotta read the river," he said.

We cooked two big rainbows over a campfire at the edge of the river. The sun was just setting red somewhere behind the trees to the west. The sunsets had been angry and red all week since most of Colorado was on fire. You couldn't go a mile down the road without seeing the No Open Fires signs.

"Can we get in trouble for having a fire?" I asked.

"Ain't no law can stop a man from cooking his dinner," Clancy snickered as he passed me a Bota Bag full of his homemade hooch. "I ever tell you how I learned to make shine?"

"I don't think so."

"My father was one of the biggest bootleggers in these parts, before I was born. His shine cabin is still standing in Golden Gate Canyon State Park, 'bout the size of yer shack. His still was the most sophisticated in all the state. He could put out a good six gallons a night of the best stump whiskey this country's ever drunk. The secret's the water. He had a crisp, cold, clear, and continuous supply of water running down from the peaks of Mount Tremont. By 1923, his whiskey had made it all the way to Chicago. It was Capone's favorite; he tried for years to get my father to open a speakeasy in Lost Creek. Father wanted no part of going into business with him. But Capone wouldn't take no for an answer and sent a beautiful walnut bar top from one of his own clubs in Chicago to Lost Creek with stern instructions that my father was to open a club immediately. Father never responded, never even went to look at the bar top Capone had sent..." Clancy paused for a long moment before taking a pull. "Dumb sonnofabitch," Clancy snickered.

"What's so funny?"

"That's how the Campbells came into power. Can't believe I never put it together."

"I don't get it."

"Terrance Campbell, the sheriff's father, he was the local law in Lost Creek, a real crooked bastard. My father used to tell me how Terrance came across the bar top during a raid and cut a deal with Capone. It was Capone who gave Terrance the money to buy the old Toll Gate Barn from the Butterfield Stage Coach Company and run it as a front for a speakeasy. The password was Wagon Wheel, that's where the name came from. Capone put up all the money to get the Campbells into government all around the county. And when my father refused to supply the Wagon Wheel, Capone stopped protecting Father's shipments. He had to paint his wagon as the Smith's Bread Wagon to throw off the lawmen and paid the local ranchers to drive their cattle behind the wagon to trample the tracks. He cooked hooch from '21 till '33, when they finally repealed the Eighteenth Amendment. Not a single shipment was ever stopped."

The sun was already setting over the Divide and Clancy was hammered when he finished his story — not that I wasn't a bit tipsy. But I wasn't thrashing through the brush, tripping over trees and getting clotheslined by low-hanging branches like Clancy — okay, I might have tripped over a tree root and fallen face first into a pile of elk turds. Clancy got a real kick out of that — he fell over he was laughing so hard. Blue looked at us like we were a couple of idiots gone mad. It was dark by the time we stumbled back to my shack. I insisted Clancy stay. He tried to put up a fight, but he could hardly mumble the words. Then, as soon as we walked through the door, Clancy seemed to immediately sober up. He knelt in the corner and stared silently at the window. Thinking of Martin brought back the realization from his prior story. He had been hit with a whole new reason, dating back to before he was born, why it was his fault that Martin had died. He didn't get a wink of sleep the whole night.

Clancy was right back to his ornery old self by sunrise. I remember being so relieved when I heard him gather his things and stumble out the door. I was just about to drift back to sleep when a gunshot wrenched me out of bed. Clancy stomped back in as I was frantically trying to put on my pants.

"What the hell!?" I shouted.

"'Bout time you get up." Clancy dangled a dead rabbit just above Blue's nose.

"Why?"

"I was up all night trying to solve your problem; least you could do is pretend to appreciate."

"My problem?" I asked, thinking he was talking about the Campbells.

Clancy knew exactly why I was confused, but he continued right into his plan to get the "Feds" off my back over my student loans.

"You got credit cards?" Clancy asked as he ripped out the rabbit's guts.

"Yeah?"

"Got enough credit to cover yer loans?"

"I suppose."

"Pay off yer student loans with your credit cards."

"The interest is three times higher."

"Don't matter if you ain't gonna pay it."

"I want to pay it, someday."

"Why? Stick it to them slimy snakes. Their fault this country went to the shitter."

"My credit will be ruined."

"What the hell you need credit for?"

I had no answer. My whole adult life I had been told my "credit" was the most important thing I had. I never understood why. In college, I was told credit cards were the key. The trick was to use them to pay for things like gas and then pay off the balance before you accrued interest. So that's what I did. And the credit card companies just kept raising my limit. By the time the bank took my house, I had almost a hundred thousand dollars of credit and one hell of a good credit score.

Clancy's plan was starting to make sense. Especially when he told me that the government would immediately seize my property — "Not even bankruptcy will save you from them government bastards." He said it would be years before the credit card companies would get a judgment against me. "If you can't pay it off by then, bankruptcy will wipe that slate clean," Clancy laughed.

Two weeks later, my student loans were paid off and all but

one of my credit cards were maxed out. It was the end of August and the fall chill was already in the air. The days were getting shorter. The nights were getting colder. If I didn't stoke a good fire before bed, I could see my breath by morning. By Labor Day, the aspens were burning like yellow wildfire through the deep forest green that climbed the mountain across the valley. "Way them aspens changin' so early, we're in for one hell of a winter," Clancy claimed. I still don't believe Clancy could tell how bad the winter was going to be from when the leaves changed, but — I must admit — he was right.

I was able to ride the student loan distraction until early September. I had almost forgotten about the Campbells. Clancy had not forgotten. It was the first Friday in September when Clancy stopped by the shack and insisted I returned to the Wagon Wheel. I was reluctant, to say the least, but I told him I'd go.

"I just ate lunch, but I'll head up there for dinner," I assured Clancy. I actually had just eaten, but that's not why I wanted to wait. I was hoping Darla would be off by then.

After getting so ripped that I couldn't remember the drive home the last time I left the Wagon Wheel, I decided to walk. The parking lot was packed with jeeps and old pickups when I arrived. The bar was teeming with hillbillies when I crept in. Standing room only. And there was Darla, behind the bar, slinging drinks so fast she didn't see me. So, I snuck up the stairs behind one of the rushing waitresses. I had seen the stairs before, but never gone up to investigate. The upper level was set up as a dance hall. Big wooden beams vaulted the high ceiling. Wagon wheels hung from the beams like giant chandeliers. And a band was buzzing around the stage, setting up their instruments. I followed the waitress to a deck that overlooked the river and the tracks and the valley that leads to my shack and took the only open table.

The sun was burning red as it set over the Divide — a massive forest fire to the north provided great hazy red sunsets that week. I had just ordered dinner and was sipping my first beer when the coal train came whistling from the east. It rumbled by with such force it shook that old red barn. It made me think about Blue. I imagined he was waiting on his perch, at that very moment, to watch the train pass. And then I started to feel bad for Blue. I thought about Clancy's stories of Martin and Blue traveling across the state and sleeping under the stars together. Since being sucked into Clancy's conspiracy, Blue and I hadn't gone on any real hiking adventures.

"Here you are, sir. Can I get you anything else?" A sweet voice broke my stare just as the caboose was going around the bend. A sizzling ribeye was placed before me.

"Another beer, plea…" I froze when I saw it was Darla delivering my dinner.

"Thought I was gonna have to hunt you down." Darla pulled out the chair across from me and sat down.

"I… I… I'm sorry for skipping out on my tab. That's why I came… to pay you. You looked really busy when I walked in. I didn't want to bother you. I was going to stop by the bar on my way out." I rambled on like a nervous schoolboy.

"Sure you were," Darla giggled.

"No, really, I was… I swear."

"Haven't seen you for lunch. Thought you skipped town."

"No, not at all… I've just been busy with work." I quickly answered without thinking — I've never been good at lying under pressure.

"What do you do?"

"About what?" I answered, trying to buy myself enough time to think of something.

"About work."

"I try to avoid it at all cost." I have no idea where that came from, but it made Darla laugh. As soon as she laughed, all my nervousness was washed away. We talked back and forth till the red sky was black and our breath became frosty. I never even touched that beautiful steak. But I must have had at least six beers by the time the cold mountain air became too much to bear. I was desperately trying to think up an excuse for having to head home that wouldn't make me sound like a pussy when the band began to jam.

"You have to dance with me!" Darla jumped from her seat and yanked me from mine.

"I don't really dance."

"Come on."

"I really should get home; I have a long walk and it's getting cold."

"You owe me. I had to cover your lunch tab the other day out of my own pocket."

An hour later, I was a sweaty mess. I was a dancing fool — something else the me before Lost Creek would have never done. The last time I had danced with a girl was at my senior prom — an awkward affair, to say the least. I probably looked just as lost with Darla as I did back then, but the six pints of liquid courage made me oblivious — I was movin' and groovin' like I knew what I was doin'. The music was like nothing I had ever heard before. It was country; it was rock; it was jazz; it was blues — it was a funky blend as rich and diverse as the mountain folks in the crowd.

We danced and drank and smoked joints right in the middle of the dance floor till the band stopped playing — that Darla could drink. She must have downed two dozen shots of blackberry brandy before the lights shined. They had no effect. I only had about eight beers and I was ripped. We were engaged in conversation at the downstairs bar as the crowd filtered out. Darla was dripping with raw energy. She spoke with such passion and knowledge. Having never been to college, she knew a hell of a lot more than me, about everything.

Between the booze and the banter, my head was spinning when the band said their goodbyes. The night was clear and the air was crisp as Darla locked the door to the bar.

"You should let me drive you home." I slurred as I fumbled for my keys.

"You playin' pocket pool down there?"

"I can't find my keys."

"You didn't drive."

"Oh, yeah… You should let me drive you home in your car."

"Oh, really?" Darla's tone told me she had sensed my

perverse intentions.

"It's not like that. I just don't want to see you get in trouble. You had a lot more to drink than me. Let me drive you home, so I know you're safe."

"I walked to work; I'm only a mile up the hill."

"A mile!? Don't you know there's mountain lions in these parts? You gotta let me walk you home."

"Mountain lion, huh? Well, I guess I better let you walk me home," Darla mocked my pathetic proposition.

The stars were brilliant as we skipped up the hill. A sliver of moon was already setting over the Divide. And I was certain Darla was only pretending to be cold as she snuggled up tight. I was so certain, a strange confidence boiled up from unknown origins.

"You ever seen the Big Dipper?" I asked, nearly gagging as I thought about how pathetic I was to be using a line I learned from Clancy.

"Will you show it to me?" Darla smiled to let me know she was willing to play along.

I was too embarrassed to continue and turned my eyes to the southern sky rather than my crotch like Clancy had suggested. Darla let me search the stars of the southern sky for a long minute before laughing.

"The Big Dipper's that way, stud." She spun me around and pointed to the northern horizon.

"I knew that," I kidded.

"Sure you did."

"I was just getting my bearings."

"So, where's the North Star?"

"Up there?" I blindly pointed toward the Big Dipper.

"Not quite." Darla took my hand and guided my finger to the North Star. "The last two stars of the Big Dipper point straight to the North Star, which is the last star on the handle of the Little Dipper."

"Are you sure?" I joked, trying to play it off like I was kidding the whole time.

"You are too cute." Darla kissed my unsuspecting lips.

We were a tangled mess of hormones as we stumbled upon Darla's doorstep. I might have been intimidated by her massive two-story log home nestled into the hill looking over the entire valley had my senses made any sense. We were naked by the time we crashed through her front door, pawing at each other like wild animals on the tile of her entryway. We bumped our way up the steps to her bedroom in the loft. I had never felt such a connection. But, to be honest with you, I really didn't have much experience. I had one girlfriend all throughout high school. We were both virgins until that awkward first time in the backseat of my car after our senior prom. We did do a lot of practicing the summer that followed, but we never got it right. Come fall, we went off to different colleges, as friends, and never spoke again. And aside from a couple college flings, and a six-month girlfriend shortly after I moved to Minneapolis, my love life had been pretty nonexistent.

A wave of panic rushed over me as we fell onto Darla's bed. It had been over a year since I slept with a girl, let alone an experienced woman. All I could think about was how horribly disappointed Darla was going to be. And then the worry was washed away. I know all the credit belongs to Darla, she was guiding my every move, but I felt like I knew what I was doing. I felt like I was good. I felt like Darla was truly satisfied as we fell trembling to our backs as the sun was just beginning to rise.

The clock flashed noon as I awoke naked and alone. The sun was burning bright through the wall of windows overlooking Darla's bed. My head was pounding and my throat was dry. It took a few seconds to realize where I was. And then a big smile crept across my face. That was the best night of my life. I climbed out of bed and stood naked before the window looking over the brilliant valley. I felt like a changed man; I felt like a man. I was always the one to cover myself with a towel even if I was the only one in the house. I didn't even run for cover when Darla pranced up the stairs and into the loft with breakfast. In fact, I heard her coming and waited until she said, "Good morning" to turn from the window, pretending to be surprised.

Breakfast was cold by the time we got to it. Darla had cooked up a meal fit for a king: scrambled eggs (from the chickens out back), venison sausage (from a deer she shot last fall), fried potatoes and peppers (from her garden), and a big glass of orange juice (from the grocery store in Nederland) — she drove all the way down to Ned when she woke up to get me orange juice.

CHAPTER 4

Blue and I spent most of our fall with Darla. She took us all over the state. Blue wasn't too sure of Darla at first, but after a couple of great hikes, she was alright. He really enjoyed riding in the backseat of Darla's Jeep, with the breeze blowing in his face. Darla has a big Jeep that sits atop huge mud tires. We climbed a straight-up boulder field to cross the Continental Divide one crazy day. I was sure we were going to tip over backwards. Darla wasn't nervous for a second. We took a road trip to Aspen to gawk at the brilliant leaves of Independence Pass. We ripped up and over Rollins Pass on Darla's dirt bikes — that was a blast. It was the first time I had ever ridden a motorcycle. And with only one little out-of-control wobble the first time I tried to start off, I did pretty well — Darla was a good teacher. Except when she laughed when I found the powerband for the first time — that damn bike almost shot right out from between my legs. She took us to all the good bars and restaurants in Nederland — every joint let Blue come in with us. I couldn't believe it.

Speaking of joints, I was getting quite used to smoking pot. Darla didn't do anything or go anywhere without first taking a couple puffs. And, I will admit, I quite liked it. Especially after we'd hike up to some hidden rocky bluff looking high over the rolling ridges that surrounded us in every direction. One day, Darla led me to this rocky perch in Eldorado Canyon. To the east we could see the hazy city. To the west was the rigid Divide. The aspens were burning yellow and those white wispy clouds that form strange and familiar forms were slowly blowing across the brilliant blue sky. We spoke nonsense. We spoke truth — that deep-down truth that sometimes sneaks out when you suddenly find yourself too comfortable with someone. We talked for hours, about everything. I had never felt like I had ever known anyone so well. And no one had ever really known me like Darla.

I was falling for Darla, hard. I was happy. For the first time in my life, I was truly happy. That made things extra difficult whenever Clancy would come around, hounding me for samples of Darla's weed. I had already decided that I would no longer play along with Clancy's crazy conspiracy claims. It was obvious he was either making up the entire story or he was completely delusional — there was no way Darla was capable of killing anyone.

By mid-October Clancy was starting to get angry. I decided I better ask Darla if I could buy a bag before Clancy did something stupid. What's the worst that could happen? I knew she wasn't going to poison me. So, I asked her when we returned to her place after an all-day hike in Clear Creek Canyon.

"You don't have to buy it, silly."

"I don't mind."

"You're adorable." Darla trotted off down the hall from her kitchen to a steel door leading out the back of her house and returned with a baggie full of buds. "That should last you a day or two," she giggled.

I headed straight to Clancy's shack. I felt like such a schmuck handing over a bud to Clancy to have tested. I kept the rest of the bag to roll sunrise joints — Martin definitely knew a good thing when he saw it. At the same time, I was relieved. I figured Clancy could get the sample tested, find no poisons, and maybe he would give up on his crazy quest. I even had the silly notion that over time I could convince Clancy that Darla was a good person and maybe we could all spend time together.

"'Bout time," Clancy grumbled.

"Should we bring it to your professor friend?"

"We need more."

"Why?"

"You piss her off?"

"No… not yet." I had forgotten about that part of Clancy's plan.

"Then she probably didn't poison it. Ain't no sense in wastin' a trip."

"What if she did?"

"Then we got the bitch."

"But if I go back looking for more, she'll know something's up. She'll probably kill me on the spot."

Clancy sat back in his chair for a minute to scratch his beard.

"That's a good point… Can you drive me down to Boulder tomorrow?"

"Sure," I answered, knowing I was supposed to join Darla on a hike to Brainard Lake.

I raced to Darla's early the following morning to tell her I had to take care of some business down the hill and wouldn't be able to join her. I was so afraid she would ask me what it was, but, at the time, she was completely understanding and confident enough not to need to know. A serious relief, because I've never been a good liar.

I raced back to the shack just before Clancy arrived. It was a quiet trip down the hill — aside from the Accord's muffler-less rumble. We met Clancy's professor friend, Dr. Kindberg, in the chemistry lab at the Boulder campus. Kindberg was an interesting character. He had an almost Einstein-like gray nest of ratty hair on the top of his head. He looked like a real-life mad scientist, white lab coat and everything. He told Clancy it would be about a week before he had the results.

My assignment was to spend the next week at the Wagon Wheel, spouting off like an arrogant tourist in front of Darla. I did spend most of the week with Darla at the Wagon Wheel, but I was doing anything but trying to piss her off. She was already a little mad at me for ditching out on our Brainard Lake hike. She never said anything, but I could tell. The only reason she planned the trip was because I told her I had never seen a moose. "You can't go up there without seeing at least one big bull," she assured me. She hadn't had to work a single day for the prior month, until the day after I ditched out. She worked every day that entire week. And Blue and I ate lunch at the Wagon Wheel every day. By Wednesday we were right back to good.

We went to Brainard Lake the following Saturday. I saw my first moose, a big bull standing high above the tall grass at the edge of a swamp chewing willow shoots without a care in the world. His back was humped almost like a camel and stood at least seven feet tall. His antlers were like giant platters that spread six feet across. We were standing on the trail, less than fifty yards from him, listening to him moo and groan for a good half-hour. He knew we were there. He didn't care.

When we finally got to the lake it was well past lunch time. My stomach was growling. I had long worked off my dry cereal. Blue fended off his hunger by eating elk turds all the way up the trail. He knew he wasn't supposed to eat them — you could see it in his eyes when he realized he'd been caught — but he just couldn't stop. They were like crack to him. Anyway, I was just about to dig into my pack for a bag of trail mix and a couple slices of jerky when Darla pulled a feast from her pack. You should've seen that pack. I carried this little old green canvas pack of Martin's with black nylon straps that cut into my shoulders; she carried a giant nylon pack, with big padded straps, that hung higher than the top of her head and went all the way down to her cute little butt. The thing was heavier than her. She always packed a half-dozen layers for different temperatures, enough food and water for three days, extra socks, rain gear, a first aid kit, flashlight, toilet paper — and that was just her daypack. Anyway, she had packed us a whole picnic lunch. She had plates. She had forks. And she had knives. She had sliced the prime rib from the Wagon Wheel's dinner special the night before and piled it high on fresh rolls she baked that very morning. She even packed two bottles of IPA. And they were still cold. She felt bad for giving me the cold shoulder.

A peanut-butter sandwich tastes gourmet after a hike like that — you simply can't imagine how wonderful such an elaborate spread tasted. And I felt guilty the whole time. Darla had gone to such measures to apologize for something she had no reason to apologize for — I had lied to her. I was secretly going behind her back and having her pot tested for poisons because some crazy old mountain man told me she was a serial killer — I wasn't worthy.

Blue and I spent that night and the next few at Darla's. I told myself I was trying to make up for my deceitful ways, but I was just trying to avoid Clancy. I think it was a Wednesday that Blue and I returned to the shack. Darla had to go to the Wagon Wheel for a couple hours to do inventory and call in her liquor order. It was to be a quick trip, in and out. I just wanted to make sure the shack hadn't burned down and that no wild animals had gotten in to tear the place up and eat all my food.

"Where the hell you been?' an angry voice grumbled from the porch as we approached.

Blue charged, barking and growling, until he realized it was Clancy.

"Just taking Blue for a morning hike," I finally replied once my heartbeat returned to normal.

"We wasted a whole week, thank you very much."

"You talk to Kindberg?"

"Yep."

"No poison?"

"Nope."

"Sorry."

"I suppose you spent all the gold money?"

"No, I still have most of it." And I did. Darla never let me pay for anything.

"Well, what the hell ya waitin' for?"

"You want me to head up there right now and try to get some?"

"You got somethin' better to do?"

"Nope," I honestly answered. I couldn't think of anything

better than going back to the Wagon Wheel to see Darla. I was out the door before Clancy could say another word.

I was able to avoid Clancy for almost a week before he dropped by to demand the next sample. It was a cold and rainy late-fall day. Thick gray clouds rolled into the valley like an avalanche running down the mountain. They rolled right in and engulfed the shack just as Blue and I sat on the porch to catch the sunrise. The mornings had been cold for about a month. I was already in the habit of dressing under the covers before climbing out of bed. But that morning was damp and frigid. The wind blew the icy rain sideways and the porch roof lent no protection. It felt like a Minnesota fall — except we were actually in the clouds. I couldn't even see my car parked thirty yards from the shack through the thick, swirly, wet gray. Blue and I both agreed to stoke the fire and skip our morning hike. It took nearly three hours to warm the shack enough to shake that damp chill. And then I found myself enjoying the rain. The pattering on the tin roof became a soothing song, mixed with the crackling fire. Blue's claws click-clacked across the wood floor. Then the rubber doggie door would flap, followed by a whistling cold draft.

"In or out, Blue," I'd cry as I looked over to see him sticking his head out the door. He'd turn and grumble and click-clack back to his corner. He was back and forth for a good two hours before finally giving up on the rain relenting. Then he was sound asleep, yipping and whining and wagging and running in some sunny-day dream. And I just sat there in front of the stove, staring into the crackling fire, thinking, really thinking, for the first time ever. It's amazing how far the mind can wander without modern distractions. I think that was the first time I realized how sad my life before the mountains truly was. It was a strange realization. On one hand, I felt like I had just had some major life-altering epiphany. On the other, I was sad about all the precious time wasted rushing. I felt betrayed by my parents. Everything they taught me was wrong. I was to the point of furious about the way I had been brought up to believe that money and possessions were more valuable than knowledge when Clancy busted through the door. He was sopping wet. He was wearing his elk hide pants and matching poncho-thingy that make him look like an Indian from a 1960s cowboy show. He said his mother made it for his father. He said she was a full-blooded Navajo Indian. The first time I saw the outfit it was a light leather color that matched his floppy cowhide hat. That afternoon, they were saturated to black. He was miserably cold, but he wouldn't admit it — he still insisted the outfit was waterproof.

"Gotta come out in the rain and risk pneumonia just to find you."

"Sorry, she's been out of pot all week," I lied.

"Would it kill you to stop by and let me know how things are going?"

"I was gonna drop by today, as soon as the rain stopped."

"You get any?"

"Last night," I quickly answered with a smile. Two more weeks and this would all be over, I thought as I handed Clancy a bud. I figured I'd get him one more bud in about a week and then wait for the final results to come back negative. I felt three samples would be enough and I could finally tell Clancy I was done — maybe he would even decide to give up on his own.

"Let's head down the hill!" Clancy sang.

"Now?"

"You got a date?"

"No…" I laughed at such a silly notion, knowing Darla was set to pick me up at six for dinner in Nederland.

Driving in the clouds is not as fun as it sounds. I couldn't see twenty yards past my front bumper. The rain turned to a light drizzle halfway down the pass, accumulating on the windshield at a strange rate that no setting of the wipers could accommodate. And Clancy's waterlogged leathers were fogging the windows faster than the defroster could blow. Hairpin curves sprung out of nowhere. The pavement glistened as if it had frozen over. I was sure we were going to sail over the edge — I had nightmares about sailing over cliffs after that trip.

It was almost seven by the time we made it back to Lost

Creek. I dropped Clancy off at the end of his driveway and raced back to my place to find Darla waiting on the porch. I blamed the slick roads for my tardiness, which was somewhat true. Darla accepted and we climbed into her Jeep and drove down the hill into Ned for dinner and a movie. We ate dinner at a fancy German restaurant called the Black Forest. The food, though strange, was delightful. After dinner, we rushed over to the liquor store to pick up a six-pack of beer before catching a movie at the local theater — they let us bring in our beer. And we spent every waking moment together for the next five days. I didn't leave her company until Sunday; Darla and the rest of the Campbell clan go to church, every Sunday, no matter what.

Darla dropped me and Blue off on the way to church and I rushed straight over to Clancy's as soon as her Jeep was out of sight. There was no one home. I was just about to head back to my shack when Blue's nose turned to the wind. Clancy was approaching from the east.

"Thought you said you pissed her off?" were the first words out of Clancy's mouth.

I knew he had gotten the results.

"I thought I did."

"Not enough."

"I'm sorry. I'll head over there right now and make a complete ass out of myself."

"Just go home." His tone was not that of anger; it was of disappointment. And it really messed with my head. It seems I was mentally prepared to anger Clancy, but I couldn't handle being a disappointment.

"I can do it. I'll really piss her off this time. I'll get us another sample tonight. We can go down to Boulder first thing in the morning."

"Go home!"

"Are you mad at me?"

"I ain't mad. There's a storm blowin' in. If you don't leave now, I'll be stuck with you for the next two days."

"Storm? There's not a cloud in the sky."

Clancy hobbled onto his porch without saying another word

and slammed his door. I got to my shack just as the first flakes began to fly.

CHAPTER 5

Winter blew in with wicked force. I woke up surrounded by some strange static energy. The inside of the shack was glowing with magnificent light. I think it was late October, maybe November. Even time is lost out here. All I know is that the window was frosted over with thick white crystals. And it was freezing in the shack. Normally, up to that point, if I stoked the fire right before bed, it would be almost tolerable when I woke up. Not that morning. I had to pull my long johns under the covers and lie on them for a good five minutes before they were warm enough to wear. When I was finally able to crawl out of bed and start a fire, Blue was wiggly as a little puppy. I thought he was going to piss on the floor. I barely had the panel raised before Blue charged the doggie door. And he crumpled like an accordion when his head hit the flap. I tried to open the door; it wouldn't budge. We had gotten almost four feet of sloppy, wet, slushy snow — in one night. I had to tunnel out through the doggy door just to get outside. I was blinded by the light the moment I broke through. When my eyes finally adjusted to the bright mountain sun glaring off the virgin white snow, I was sure I had died in my sleep. Fluffy white pillows, two feet high, hung heavy on the pines. And somehow the mountains were even more beautiful. It was a whole new world. The sky up here was always unbelievably blue; but against the sparkly white snow, it had an almost neon glow. All traces of man and beast had been wiped clean — save one lonely rabbit track hopping across the yard.

I finally appreciated all the old crap Clancy had hauled to my shack. I bundled up in that hideous old black snowmobile suit, wool hat, Sorels, leather mittens, with Martin's snowshoes slung over my shoulder, and I ventured out into the winter wonderland. You should have seen Blue when I picked up those snowshoes — he was trembling with excitement.

Somehow the wilderness is even more peaceful when covered in a blanket of white. I still haven't figured out why. But I think it's a mental thing. I think there's actually more commotion after the storm clears. The birds are always chirping madly as soon as the sky turns blue. The squirrels go nuts, squawking at the snow for burying their stash. The heavy pillows drop from the overloaded pine boughs like mini-avalanches, whooshing till they thud down into the drifts below. The sounds are somehow perfectly muffled by the soft snow, but I think it's the mind that provides the peace. I think it all boils down to how our brains perceive color. So much white is like a Quaalude to the senses. If snow fell red, the citizens of the northern states would turn into angry warmongers every winter.

So much white seemed to have the same effect on Blue's brain — he turned into a happy puppy, bounding through the drifts and rolling in the fluffy white. It was the only time he didn't look like he was working. All seriousness left his expressions. We stomped around the property for two straight days. The river was probably the most spectacular. The water was so cold it ran black. White pillows sat atop the rocks like mushroom caps. Thin shields of crystal-clear ice covered the pools with no flow. Blue loved to shatter them like breaking glass.

Icicles were the wonder on the second day after the storm. The previous day's sun had every dark surface warmed enough to melt the snow well into the night. Icicles hung from the rafters to the ground, all the way around the shack, that second morning. The branches that had sprung free from their heavy loads sparkled with icicles. But for some, the weight was too great. Blue and I picked up broken branches for almost two hours that morning. I was already sweaty and exhausted by the time I strapped on the snowshoes to stomp around the property with Blue. We were almost to the river when Blue caught the scent of something in the air. The fur on his back bristled into a mohawk the moment his head tipped back. And just as fast, he was charging west into the breeze. I tried the inside-out whistle, to no effect. When I finally caught up to Blue, I found him circling a bush, making a strange half-growling, half-whining noise. At twenty yards away, I still couldn't see what he had cornered in the bush. That's when I met the mountain lion. The beast pounced from under a pine tree about ten yards left of Blue. He snarled and hissed as he cut the air with his paw full of razor-sharp claws. I immediately reached for the knife on my belt that Clancy said to never leave home without. My brain repeatedly told my hand to draw it, but my whole body was frozen. Blue growled, the cat snarled, and I was shaking in my boots. Blue hunched back, just about to lunge, when the cat turned tail and bounded up the hill. I was sure Blue was going to give chase, but he returned to circling his bush.

When I was finally able to move, I realized what Blue was all riled up about. There was a big ten-point buck dragged into the bush. The lion had killed it the night before and feasted throughout the night. There was nothing left but the head. I still believe, had he not been so full, the mountain lion would surely have killed me. That buck probably weighed twice what I weigh. He probably ran three times as fast. But that lion had no problem taking him down. That lion didn't even have a problem dragging that big buck for more than a hundred yards from where he killed it — we followed the drag marks all the way up the hill to where the fresh white snow was spattered with the red evidence of the kill. I felt like a crime scene investigator, following the clumps of hair to the first spatter of blood. I stomped straight back to the shack that afternoon, with my knife gripped tightly in my hand the whole way.

I didn't see Clancy again until three days after the storm. "If you can't open the door, don't leave the shack," was Clancy's response to my tunneling-out-the-doggy-door story. "That beautiful white light is the siren's song. Mother Nature loves to trick the fools into venturing out into her beauty just so she can end them with her vicious cold." I saw less and less of Clancy as the snow piled higher and higher. "The day after the storm is always the coldest." Clancy wouldn't leave his shack for days when we got back-to-back storms.

It was early morning, a few days after one of those early-winter, four-day storms that Clancy came storming into my shack.

"You get any, yet?"

"No."

"What!?"

"What do you mean, what?" I shot back. I've never been quick with rebuttals, but I knew he couldn't argue — "The 'Siren's Song,'" I smiled. That was the first time I ever really shut down Clancy — even Blue noticed.

"Can you go today?" Clancy conceded.

"I planned to, as soon as they plow Lost Creek Trail."

"They just made a pass."

"Help me dig out the Accord and I'll try to catch her before the lunch rush."

Two hours later, I was rumbling off to the Wagon Wheel. I got there just as the lunch rush was swelling. I smiled when I saw the full parking lot, knowing the crowd would buy me at least an extra hour before I had to report back to Clancy. Darla was running around like a chicken with its head cut off when I walked in. It must have taken her twenty minutes to notice I was there. But the moment she spotted me, she gave me a wink. I immediately knew it meant that she was asking if I wanted my usual and I nodded to affirm. It wasn't thirty seconds later that Darla slid a pint of IPA in front of me.

"Cheeseburger and fries?" she asked.

"You know me," I answered with a smile.

"I already put the order in," she winked.

I hadn't even finished my first pint when I spotted Clancy storm through the door. Darla and I had just decided to head down the hill to Ned when she was done with work to catch a movie.

"You sonofabitch!" Clancy screamed as he marched towards me, shaking his fist. I thought he had figured us out, at first. "You think you can take my land without a fight?" he quickly continued. The bar went silent and everyone stopped what they were doing and turned their attention to Clancy. "This flatlander's buying up all the land in Lost Creek to build town homes! He's trying to squeeze all us locals out and replace us with rich commuters and early retirees."
I didn't have to look to feel the glaring eyes surround me.

"He's lying," I cried. It came out before I had a chance to think. I could see the doubt in Darla's eyes.

"I'm lying?" Clancy roared. "He tell you guys the one about how Martin picked his name out of the phonebook?"
Darla's eyes screamed with betrayal.

"He's the one that told me that," I whispered to Darla.

"'Cause we all know Martin had stacks of out-of-state phone books lying around his shack," Clancy continued.

My head was spinning. I knew that phone book story was bullshit. Was Clancy that clever? Had he planted that little nugget with this very intent? Did he know about Darla and me this whole time? Was this his revenge? What must Darla think? I'd been so embarrassed to admit I was laid off and unemployed, I changed the subject every time Darla brought up my work. "It's boring... computer stuff," was the most I ever said.

"You ever set foot on my property, again, I'll blast off both yer kneecaps and leave you screaming till the coyotes pick yer bones clean," was the last thing Clancy cried as he stormed out the door. Even if I hadn't been able to feel the energy in the room turn negative, all I had to do was look down to see Blue's back hair bristling to know a predator was about to pounce.

"I think you should leave," Darla demanded. Her voice was stern. But her eyes looked concerned. I couldn't tell whether she had believed Clancy and didn't want to see me, or she wanted me to leave for my own safety. Her eyes gave me hope so I decided to heed her advice.

"How much do I owe you?" I reached for my wallet.

"Don't." Darla turned to the kitchen. Her eyes had lied.

I approached my shack half-expecting to be shot before I stepped onto the porch. The other half was so pissed at Clancy for screwing things up with Darla I was contemplating shooting him. I was pretty sure he hadn't found out about us and was just trying to expedite his investigation — but that didn't stop me from having a heart attack when Clancy stormed out of my shack.

"You played that brilliantly," Clancy cried as I stepped onto the porch. "That denial angle was perfect... really made you look guilty."

"You could have warned me," I finally whined back once the shock wore off.

"Didn't want it to look staged."

"You made me look like an asshole!"

"Exactly."

"That's all good and great, until she decides to shoot me."

"Nah, poison's her thing."

"So, she'll come and drug me while I'm sleeping."

"Blue'd never let her."

"Yeah, you're probably right," I answered. Yeah right, Blue would roll over and let her rub his belly, I thought. "But this is the last time. If the test comes back negative, I'm done."

Clancy quickly agreed, but I could tell he wasn't sincere. I told him I would try to get one more bag — if Darla would still speak to me. Clancy assured me she would. Knowing everything I knew, I wasn't so sure. But more than anything, I wanted to put that out there so I could use it later to hold off Clancy by telling him Darla would no longer sell to me.

A blizzard drifted three feet of crusty white snow against the shack before I crawled out of bed the next morning. All I wanted to do was strap on the snowshoes and stomp up to the Wagon Wheel to plead my case to Darla, but I had no idea what I was going to say. Somehow, I convinced myself that I would come up with the right words while digging out the Accord. Two hours later, I was sliding onto Lost Creek Trail, moments after the plow made his first pass. It was obvious, before I had even made it a mile, that the Accord had no business on such sketchy roads. That's what I said to convince myself to drive right past the Wagon Wheel, anyway. I was convinced I couldn't survive without a four-wheel-drive. I would have told myself anything to avoid facing Darla. An hour later, I was in Denver, trading the Accord for an old Toyota pickup. The truck was in rough shape — even compared to the Accord — but it had four-wheel-drive and studded snow tires. I had never even heard of snow tires, let alone studded tires. As bad as the winter roads were in Minnesota, I never knew of anything other than all-season tires. I now count that as a blessing: learning to drive on bald all-season tires on the icy roads of Minnesota taught me to handle these curvy mountain roads, on proper tires, with the greatest of confidence.

My confidence on the road did not translate to my personal life. I thought about what I was going to say to Darla the whole way up the hill. I thought about coming clean. I thought about keeping the lie alive. I thought I was going to drop by the Wagon Wheel. But I drove right on by. I had no idea what to say. And somehow I was able to convince myself that I needed to immediately build a snow freezer behind my shack. Clancy had told me to do so after the first snowfall. So I dropped down the other side of the mountain to get some groceries in Ned. I loaded up on frozen chicken breasts and fruits and vegetables — I was getting sick of elk jerky.

I spent almost two hours digging and packing the snow behind my shack. I packed a nice flat base and poured a bucket of water over it to turn it to ice, just like Clancy said. I packed the walls hard and thick and iced them down. Getting the roof formed was a bit tougher than Clancy led me to believe, but I finally thought to span the gap with a pine bow and pile snow on top. It was nearly dark by the time my freezer was formed. I threw in my chicken, blocked the opening, and piled snow against it. I hung all the vegetables, except what I was planning to eat right away, in a bag on the porch to let them freeze overnight.

I cooked myself quite a feast over the barrel stove that night. I boiled a pot of water for pasta on top of the barrel. I made a marinara sauce with fresh tomatoes, red and yellow peppers, squash, and onion. I steamed broccoli over the pasta water in one of Martin's old stainless-steel sand scoops — normally used for gold panning. I grilled two chicken breasts right on the grate in the stove. I even warmed a loaf of garlic bread over the hot coals. And I was only doing all of this because of some secret plan, deep in my subconscious, to keep myself from seeing Darla. I had told myself, as soon as I finished dinner, I would head to the Wagon Wheel and tell Darla the truth. It was the right thing to do. And then I piled enough food to feed three of me onto one of Martin's old gold pans and gorged myself. I knew I would never leave the shack after a meal like that. I even gave Blue a whole breast; he was full, fat, satisfied, and sound asleep in front of the fire by the time my plate was clean.

After dinner, I convinced myself I couldn't leave my shack before cleaning up my mess. I'll smoke a joint, wash the dishes, and then I'll go up to the Wagon Wheel, I told myself. I did smoke a joint. I did not wash the dishes. And I did not go the Wagon Wheel.

I was up before the sun the following morning. My vegetables were nice and frozen as I sparked one for the sunrise. When the morning's colors were finally bled from the sky, I decided I better pack my frozen produce in my snow freezer before heading up to talk to Darla. The chore took far less time than I had hoped. I figured I had better wash up the dishes before I left. Taking Blue for a much-deserved hike was the next excuse. I strapped on the snowshoes and let Blue lead me on a three-hour adventure. But even the calm of the white wilderness couldn't settle my mind.

I finally forced myself to go when we returned. I still had no idea what I was going to say as I rumbled my new truck down Lost Creek Trail. Suddenly, after procrastinating for so long, I found myself in a hurry when I noticed the clock on the radio flashing fifteen after nine. I kicked the pedal and fishtailed, hoping I could catch Darla at her house before she went down to open the bar — she normally left her house at about nine-thirty. It was nine-twenty when I roared up to the intersection. Darla was already walking down the hill as I crossed the highway. She was just unlocking the front door as I parked the truck. My spirits were lifted for a brief moment when I saw her smile at me. Then I realized she had no idea it was me behind those dark-tinted windows of my new truck.

My concern was confirmed when I humbly stumbled to a stool at the bar. Darla wouldn't even look at me.

"Burger and a beer, sir?" she asked like she didn't even know me.

"Can we talk?"

She scurried off to the kitchen without reply. It seemed like years before the kitchen door crashed open to announce her return.

"You want a beer or what?" Darla rushed past with an armload of condiments.

"Why are you doing this?"

"Doing what?" She returned. "I'm just busy." Her angry energy washed over me and my subconscious took over.

"Are you kidding me?" I fired back. "You're just gonna let what some crazy old man said ruin what we have?" I continued, spewing words my conscious had never heard.

I laid into Darla for a good ten minutes. By the time I finally shut up, I had almost convinced myself that everything was Darla's fault. I was actually scolding her for believing crazy old Clancy over me by the time I finished. When I finally gave her a chance to respond, she told me she believed me. But the next words from her mouth were, "We shouldn't see each other anymore." Suddenly, she felt the age difference between us was too great.

I stomped out of the Wagon Wheel like a two-year-old having a tantrum. I pouted the whole way back to the shack. Even Blue's delight to see me couldn't change my mood. I was so angry, I let Clancy's conspiracy cloud my judgment. I spent the entire day stoking the fire and convincing myself that Darla was a killer. How else could she just throw away what we had shared? By the time the sun set, I was certain she was going to kill me.

The following morning, my mission was clear. I was going to get Clancy his evidence. I told Blue we were going for a ride, and I drove straight to Darla's. I was pounding on her front door at first light. I thought she would be angry that I came so early; maybe I was just hoping she would be to make my mission of deception easier, but her innocent blue eyes sparkled and a sweet smile spread across her face the moment she opened the door. It really threw me off.

"I know you hate me, but can I buy some pot from you? I can't sleep," I finally muttered, much less dramatically than I had practiced the whole way there.

"I don't hate you."

"Really?"

"I don't."

"So, you'll sell me a bag?"

"Do you believe me?"

"Sure."

"I don't believe you."

I didn't know what to say. I actually *did* believe her. The pathetic look on her face was a dead giveaway. Her innocent blue eyes couldn't possibly lie. And they quickly sucked my confidence. My plan flared then fizzled before my mind's eye like a sparkler dipped in water. I was more confused than ever. I was the biggest asshole in the world.

"I should leave."

"Please don't."

I didn't. Instead, Blue and I followed Darla into her kitchen like a couple of lost puppies looking for a bone. And we both got exactly what we were looking for. Blue got his in the kitchen. He was still gnawing at it when I got mine in the loft. My worries were washed away. I felt so silly for letting my emotions drag me back into Clancy's conspiracy. But that didn't stop me from jabbing Darla for tossing me to the curb over the crazy rants of the madman known as Clancy.

"I don't think I can see you," I giggled as I fumbled for my long johns. "Clancy says you were just released from the nuthouse... Everything Clancy says is true," I kidded.

Darla was a puddle with puppy dog eyes by the time we left for the bar. I had never done that before. I had never in my life been able to play that game. And I think it changed me a little. I felt this strange power, for the first time, like I had just learned a whole new angle. Conversations, relationships, any interactions, really, could all be shaped and molded to bear the exact outcome you are hoping for if you simply project the outcome in your mind. I felt like some sort of genius. I felt dirty.

"I'm sorry," Darla kept saying as I walked her down the hill. And every time she said it, I felt a little worse. All I could think about was how she would have no need to apologize had I just been honest with her from the beginning. At the same time, I felt this awkward sense of superiority over her. I had never felt that before. I felt like I had broken a wild mare and she was now mine to saddle.

"I forgive you." I kissed her as she unlocked the door to the bar.

"You comin' in?"

"No... I've got some things to take care of," I said, thinking about stomping straight to Clancy's and telling him to go to hell.

"You wanna come over for dinner?"

"How about you come over to my place and let me cook you dinner?"

"Yeah?"

"Yeah."

Blue and I left the Wagon Wheel and drove straight down into Nederland for groceries and cleaning supplies. I think Blue thought I was mad at him after I practiced telling off Clancy the whole way down the hill. But, by the time I got back to my shack, I had convinced myself the confrontation could wait. I decided making my shack presentable for Darla was a much higher priority. Her place was always spotless when she had me over. I spent the whole afternoon cleaning my shack. After four hours of scrubbing years of waxy grease from every surface, I was really starting to regret inviting Darla to dinner. I spent another hour trying to sweep fifty years of sand out of the cracks between the floorboards. I could have filled a sandbox by the time I was done — and the cracks were still full.

When the sun finally set red to the west, I stopped worrying. The fact that my little lantern didn't expose the dirt had a bit to do with my relief — the sunset joint may have also been a factor — but I think it was the fact that I knew it was too late for Clancy to drop by that really set my mind at ease. I worried all day about Clancy coming over and questioning the motive behind my cleaning spree. And even if I could explain that, I had no excuse for the two big ribeye steaks marinating on the table.

I told Darla to come over at seven-thirty, knowing Clancy would never stop by after dark. She was right on time. The shack was radiating with warmth when I opened the door to Darla and the cold wind. I had stoked the fire all afternoon — burning up two night's worth of wood.

"Someone cleans up nice," Darla whistled as she stepped in and brushed her soft, cold fingers across my cheek. I had bought a razor and shaving cream and shaved the scruffy beard off my face for the first time in months — a horrible and bloody experience that I haven't repeated since.

"You sure do," I winked. "Can I take your coat?"

"And he's a gentleman." Darla handed me a bottle of wine.

"I wouldn't go that far. I don't even have the tools to open this for you," I smiled as I took the bottle.

I was feeling a bit vulnerable as I took Darla's jacket. I remember looking over my dirty shack as I hung her coat on the corner of the bookshelf and thinking how pathetic the place must look — Darla's kitchen was bigger than the entire shack.

"So, this is your place?" Darla asked. "I like it," she said with such sincerity my confidence was replenished.

"Would you like a tour?" I joked.

"I would."

I took Darla's arm and spun in a circle.

"Living room, bedroom, kitchen… and shower," I giggled,

pointing to the bucket on the wall.

"It's perfect."

I was just about to come back with something about how *not* perfect my situation was when I realized she was right. I couldn't imagine a better setting.

"It is… except I don't have a corkscrew." I smiled, holding up the bottle of wine.

"No corkscrew? Well, I'm outta here," Darla said with complete seriousness as she grabbed her coat.

The defeat on my face must have been glaring.

"I'm kidding," Darla laughed. "Gimme that." Darla pulled a Swiss Army knife from her purse — which was more like a small backpack — and popped the cork. "You got any glasses?"

"Glasses I can handle," I said before realizing the old Mason jars I had been using for drinking glasses were probably not the proper glassware for Darla's top-shelf wine. My embarrassment over handing Darla a small round jelly jar was immediately extinguished by the smile on Darla's face.

"Ain't no wine finer than that drunk from a jar," Darla toasted. I was certain she only said it to make me feel better — it worked. And she continued to feed my ego. "Smells absolutely heavenly in here."

"Thank you."

"Is that garlic?"

"It is."

My baby red potatoes were sizzling over the orange embers in the belly of the stove. Martin had welded brackets inside the barrel that held a grill grate just above the flames. I found that if I rolled baby red potatoes in olive oil and sprinkled them with garlic I could cook them right on the grate — they came out of the fire like little mashed potato balls with a crunchy garlic shell.

We had nearly polished off the whole bottle of wine by the time I realized I had completely screwed up the timing. The potatoes were almost done, and I hadn't even put the steaks on the stove. And because I was trying to show off, I also bought a yellow squash that I had no idea how to prepare. I ended up slicing it into little round slabs about a quarter-inch thick, brushing them with olive oil and sprinkling them with garlic and oregano. I cooked them right on the grate with the steak, flipping them at the same time — they were the best part of the meal, aside from the company.

The shack was blue with smoke before the dishes were done — Darla rolled two fat joints and told me to stoke the fire, smoke a joint, and relax while she smoked one and washed the dishes. I wanted to tell her I'd do it in the morning, but, even more, I wanted to get stoned and relax — I said nothing and did as I was told.

I was pretty well ripped when Darla curled up to me in front of the fire. We must have talked for hours, lit by the crackling flames. I found myself telling things to Darla that I've never told anyone, things I had been too ashamed to admit, things I had never even admitted to myself. By the time we killed the twelve-pack of Darla's favorite beer that I bought, I was spilling my whole pathetic story of being teased and tormented throughout high school. I told Darla all about how the football players got off by pulling my pants down in front of the other classmates. I even told her about the time I thought I had gotten smart and bought a belt, so they couldn't "pants" me. She looked so sympathetic when I told her my plan backfired. She didn't even laugh when I told her how my pants ripped at the seams and I was left standing before the entire auditorium with nothing but my belt loops and front pockets hanging from my new belt. Darla did giggle a bit when I admitted to wearing smiley-face Joe Boxers on that fateful day.

Darla was just as generous. Her sad stories revolved around her parents. Her despair was born from never leaving the county. It seems her folks would not allow it. Darla's high school story was much different from mine. She was one of the popular girls. She was an "A" student. She was a star athlete. She excelled at every sport she tried, but skiing was her favorite. She was offered a full scholarship to ski for the University of Colorado. Her folks forbade her. Her entire life had already been carefully planned out by her father — and that plan had most certainly been passed down by her grandfather. Darla was destined to run the Wagon Wheel before she was even born.

But before she let herself give away all the family secrets, she returned to skiing. It was a topic that really lit her face. It was obvious there was nothing in this world that she would rather do.

"Tomorrow's opening day," Darla's face glowed.

"Opening day?"

"Eldora… tomorrow's opening day. That's where I learned to ski. We gotta go."

"I don't know how to ski."

"It's easy. I'll teach you."

"I don't have skis."

"I have relatives in every department; you won't need to buy a thing."

"Okay."

"You're gonna have to get up at first light, you think you can handle that?"

"Yeah."

"You think you can handle it if I spend the night?" Darla winked.

"Oh, I can handle it." I blew out the lantern.

I was truly excited to climb under the covers with Darla, but, even more, I'm ashamed to admit, I was relieved that I wouldn't have to come up with an excuse about why we had to leave the shack shortly after sunrise — I was worried Clancy would drop by to find us.

The night bled into morning, with Blue grumbling about the moaning. I don't remember going to sleep, but I remember waking up. The shack was sizzling with warmth and a peppery maple aroma.

"Chairs turn in an hour," Darla hollered.

"Chairs?" I looked out from the covers to see Darla flipping a skillet over the stove. "What are you talking about, chairs turn?" I had completely forgotten about agreeing to go skiing.

"Come get some breakfast. You're going to need it." Darla had snuck out while I was still sleeping and raided the Wagon Wheel kitchen. She served me up a big plate of scrambled eggs, bacon, diced peppers, fried potatoes, and a steaming cup of hot coffee as I sat up in bed.

We we're buzzing up the steep and curvy road to Eldora in Darla's Jeep, at breakneck speeds, passing a joint back and forth long before breakfast had a chance to settle. There was no getting out of this commitment. I couldn't even slow Darla down to delay the inevitable embarrassment. She was on a mission. We marched straight to the rental office after we parked. Darla said a few quick words to the guy behind the desk and he was quickly fitting me with top of the line gear. The next stop was the retail store. Darla said she wouldn't allow me to hit the slopes wearing Martin's black snowsuit with the bright orange stripes. The saleswoman dressed me from head to toe with the best accessories, socks to hat, gloves, parka, pants, and goggles. It didn't cost us a dime. With my free season pass hanging from my brand-new jacket, we hit the slopes.

Getting on the chairlift was a breeze. It was just the boost my shaky confidence needed. The sky was blue and bright. The sun was high and hot. But the air had the perfect chill that seemed to somehow cleanse the lungs with every breath. The view from the chairlift was magnificent. The mountain ranges slowly rolled smaller on their way to the open plain where a hazy grey confusion could only be the city. My attempt at getting off the chairlift brought me right back to reality. I was skidding and hopping and waving my poles in the air like a lunatic. And then I crashed into the trashcan. I was ready to give up after flailing for a good five minutes just to get back on my feet. Darla was laughing her ass off.

"I think we better stick to the greens," Darla joked when she finally helped me up.

Green means easy — my ass. I thought I was going to die at least a dozen times on my first run alone. As hard as I tried to stay in the middle of the run and make nice gradual turns like Darla instructed, my skis sent me barreling for the trees. Back and forth, I raced until I reached the edge and crashed to avoid smacking a tree — I couldn't stop those damn skis. It was one of the best days of my life. Sailing down the mountain provided one of the biggest rushes I had ever felt, up to that point, anyway. Darla said I was a natural. She followed me down the mountain, time after time, giving me tips along the way. I could tell it was not Darla's idea of a fun day on the mountain. It was killing her to go so slow. Every once and a while she would get sick of waiting and zip down a pitch, fly off a jump, and spin a three-sixty at full speed. Then she would skid to a stop and patiently wait for me. I think the fact that she was so good really made me push myself. By the end of the day, I followed Darla down the blue run. It wasn't pretty — I spent more time chasing my skis down the hill than riding them — but I made it. And I instantly understood the glow in her eyes that first time I heard her talking about skiing. I was addicted the first time I linked two turns.

Darla and I were pretty much inseparable after that day. We skied every day. We welcomed every cloud that rolled over the Divide, hoping it would dump fresh fluffy snow for us to ride. Blue and I spent weeks at a time at Darla's. And I was able to hold off Clancy's attacks by telling him Darla would no longer sell to me after his fiasco. Looking back, I feel really guilty for making Clancy believe he was the one who screwed up our plan. I convinced him they wouldn't even let me into the Wagon Wheel. All the while, Darla and I were dancing away most evenings on the Wagon Wheel's dance floor. I hardly spent a single night in the shack during December.

CHAPTER 6

It was two days before Christmas Eve when Darla invited me to spend Christmas Day with her family. I accepted immediately. Then, I thought about it all night. I hadn't seen Clancy all month. I imagined he had gone completely mad and forgotten to eat. I pictured myself finding his frozen body after forgetting to feed his fire for far too long. I figured, at the very least, I owed Clancy a decent Christmas Eve dinner for all he had done for me. I spent the entire next day hunting and gathering to present a feast for Clancy. Blue helped me scare up a couple of rabbits. I cleaned them up just like Clancy had taught me and slow-cooked them over the fire just like Clancy liked. I also boiled up a big batch of Minnesota wild rice with onions and carrot slices and baked up some baby reds over the fire.

Clancy was a mess when I got to his shack. He was drunk off his ass. He was a raving lunatic. His bed was overturned and leaning against the wall. The entire floor was littered with papers, pictures, and old newspaper clippings.

"Where the hell you been?" Clancy said with almost no emotion as he rushed about the piles, never once stopping to look at me.

"I've been around."

"Thought you were dead," Clancy's tone turned somber. It

never even crossed my mind that Clancy might think I was missing or that Darla had killed me.

"I'm sorry... I've been skiing."

"Someone's lookin' fancy," Clancy grumbled after finally stopping to look at me.

Like an idiot, I was wearing my new ski pants and jacket.

"I made your favorite," I held up the rabbit to change the subject.

"Shouldn't kill rabbits this time of year."

I decided to stop talking and set the table.

Clancy devoured his dinner without speaking a word. I don't think he had eaten in days. The moment he shoveled the last fork-full into his mouth, he stormed back to his piles and mumbled nonsense as I cleared the table.

"I finally scored a bag from Darla..." Clancy didn't even look. "We can bring it down to Boulder the day after Christmas." He didn't flinch. I tossed the bag on the table and walked out the door.

The next day was Christmas. All of Darla's relatives had gathered at her parent's house. It was right up the road from Darla's place, at the top of the hill. The driveway was packed with Jeeps and giant pickups when we finally arrived. It was a massive home overlooking the entire valley. It was sided with big, rough-sawn pine slabs that had weathered black over a hundred and some years. Darla's father greeted us at the door, in full uniform, holstered gun, badge, and even his hat. Even without the gun and uniform, Sheriff Campbell would have been scary. He stood an impressive six-foot-five. Darla said he was pushing seventy, but he had the build of a thirty-year-old linebacker.

"You have a beautiful home, sir," I sputtered as the sheriff ushered us in.

"That's kind of you to say." The sheriff would later tell me it was originally the owner of the Butterfield Stage Coach's home — for a short period. It seems Mr. Butterfield had a tragic accident shortly after the house was completed. The entry opened into the great room, with the kitchen on the left. Darla's mother, Betty, a rough-looking woman who looked more like she was in her nineties rather than late sixties, was hobbling across the quartz slab floor of the kitchen. Her skin was dark and spotted from years of harsh mountain sun. Her silver hair was so thin you could see her scalp. She labored back and forth between the stove and the fridge with obvious pain.

The house was dark and creepy from the outside, but the inside was warm and cozy. Everything was wood, lightly finished white pine, from the floor to the ceiling — except the stone fireplace that climbed all the way to the high ceiling. The home was bright and open and carefully decorated like a Swiss Alps ski chalet. The only thing creepy on the inside — aside from a few of Darla's relatives — were all the horrified heads of dead elk and deer, bear and boar, and countless other mounts hanging on every wall — there was even a taxidermied squirrel climbing a branch above the toilet.

I was swarmed with Campbells as the sheriff led me into the great room. I met the mayor of Lost Creek, two councilmen, a judge, a few contractors, and a dozen business owners. They were all Campbells. I met Darla's older brother, Bill, next in line to be sheriff — he looked just like his father. The family had their hands in all levels of government and just about every business from Black Hawk to Nederland — they owned all of Lost Creek. Except for a couple of Darla's suspicious cousins, and a few flatlander jokes, everyone was very friendly. It was the best Christmas I could remember. That may be due to the fact that there wasn't a drink in the house that wasn't spiked. The big silver coffee urn was mixed fifty-fifty with coffee and Darla's cousin's whiskey. The punch was full of 'Potka' — Darla's other cousin's pot-infused vodka. I can't remember what was in the apple cider, but it kicked like rocket fuel. The green sugar cookies, they weren't dyed for the holiday, they were baked full of ganja. The whole house was drunk and jolly long before Betty could present her spread.

We played hilarious games after dinner. The one that really helped get me in with the family was the gift exchange game. I don't remember exactly how it went, but I know everybody brought a gift and put it in the middle — we were all sitting in a big circle around the great room. We rolled two die, trying for pairs. If you rolled pairs, you got to pick a present from the middle or steal a present from someone else if they had already opened something you liked. Knowing nothing about the game, I didn't bring a present to put in the middle. Fortunately, Darla was prepared and brought one for me. It was the hit of the night. Jerry was the first one to open it. After shaking a dozen packages, he heard the bottles clanging inside the box "I brought" and quickly took it back to his seat. His face lit up when he found a full case of PBR's.

"No one's takin' this from me," he joked as he slid it out of sight under his chair.

"Tell him to look inside," Darla whispered in my ear. And after she nudged me a couple times to do so, I did.

"No way, bro!" Jerry yipped as he pulled a bottle from the case. It was a brown bottle with a duct-tape label. HONEY HOP ALE was scribbled across the tape in black magic marker. "I thought this stuff was history." Jerry was nearly in tears. "This is from you?" Jerry stared at me.

"He found it in Martin's shack when he moved in," Darla quickly cut in. "I told him you guys would appreciate it," she continued. Darla would later tell me Honey Hop Ale was a beer that her uncle, Old Man Charlie, brewed in his shack, just down the road from my place, for almost sixty years. He died two years prior. It was thought that the last beers of his last batch were drunk at a celebration outside the Wagon Wheel on his birthday the following year. Darla said Old Man Charlie was a local legend. He was Sheriff Campbell's younger brother. Besides his beer, Old Man Charlie was known for never taking or tendering a single cent his whole life. He didn't believe in money. He even got his land in Lost Creek because of a long-forgotten Land Claim law they forgot to take off the books. He brewed beer all summer long to trade for goods and services to get him through the winter. He brewed his beer with water straight from Lost Creek and used locally grown grains he traded his beer to get.

I was the hero of Christmas. Charlie's beer was stolen back

and forth between the family until Betty's oven timer finally dinged to announce the end of the game. Everyone was a little suspicious when the timer rang just after the sheriff finally rolled doubles and stole the beer from Jerry, but no one said a word. Sheriff Campbell handed a beer to Darla, the three other cousins that were stealing the case every time they rolled doubles, and then he handed one to me before disappearing with the case.

Everyone scattered when the game was over. Darla scurried off to help her mother clean the kitchen. I was left alone in the middle of the living room as her aunts, uncles, cousins, and siblings formed small groups in the corners. It was one of those awkward moments where you know you look silly standing by yourself in the middle of the room, but there's not a group in sight you feel comfortable approaching.

"Good stuff, huh?" Sheriff Campbell snuck up and patted me on the back.

"Sure is," I hacked out my answer after choking on my last swig. It truly was the best beer I have ever tasted.

"You got any brothers, Jack?" the sheriff continued.

"One."

"Older or younger?"

"Three years younger."

"You two close?"

"Yeah, I guess… He's my brother."

"Exactly! … He's your brother. You'd probably hate him if he wasn't, but you'd do anything for him because he is."

"I don't know that I'd hate him."

"You wouldn't catch me crossing the street to piss on Charlie if he was on fire, if he wasn't my brother. He was a real pain in my ass."

"You look dry," Darla stepped in to hand me a beer.

"Perfect timing," I swigged the last of the suds before handing her my empty bottle.

"Daddy?" Darla handed a beer to her father.

"I've got backup." Sheriff Campbell almost let out a laugh as he pulled a bottle of Honey Hop from his back pocket.

"You always do." Darla gave me a quick wink to ask me if I

needed to be saved from her father. I smiled back to let her know I was just fine — I had never been so in tune with another person. And I had never been so comfortable around the parents of someone I was dating — not that I'd had much experience. My high school girlfriend was the only girl I had dated long enough to meet the parents — and Sheriff Campbell had already spoken to me more than her father did in all the years we dated.

"Thanks again for the Honey Hop, Jack," The sheriff popped the cap to bring me out of my head.

"You're welcome. Thanks for letting me spend Christmas with you and your family, sir."

"Cut the 'sir' shit, Jack... My friends call me Sheriff."

"Merry Christmas, Sheriff." I raised my bottle.

"Merry Christmas, Jack." Sheriff clinked his bottle against mine.

Sheriff and I took long pulls and surveyed the room. It was so warm and friendly. I didn't even have to look at the sheriff to feel his smile. We must have been silent for minutes, but it wasn't at all awkward. It was, however, different. The whole house was bustling with family, happy family. They almost seemed to be glowing with some sort of energy that compounded as they came together. I had never felt such a powerful family bond. My past family Christmases were never more than my parents and grandparents, and maybe a couple cousins, in the very early years.

"What were we talkin' bout," Sheriff broke the silence.

"Charlie, he was a pain in your ass."

"Well, Holy Shit, Jack, I think I might like you."

"I think I might like you, too, Sheriff."

"No, seriously," Sheriff stepped in close. "Nobody listens anymore. Not sure they ever did. Folks is so concerned 'bout what they wanna say, these days, they can't be bothered to listen."

"I've always been more of a listener than a talker."

"Smart boy, Jack."

"I don't know about that. To be honest with you, I think it's the exact opposite... I rarely feel smart enough to voice my opinion."

"You already learned what most never do."

"What's that?"

"None of us know shit about shit. I was much older than you when I finally realized that."

"Jack!" Jerry drunkenly shouted a whisper.

Sheriff and I both looked over at the same time to see Jerry puffing an imaginary joint and waving me over. Sheriff watched my face flush pale white and smiled.

"Go have some fun, Jack." Sheriff patted me on the back and walked away.

It was outside on the back deck that I met Mike, another of Darla's cousins. He had just opened the new Medical Marijuana Dispensary in Lost Creek. He and Jerry invited me out to sample a new strain he called Moonlight Delight. I thought a skunk had snuck onto the deck when Mike popped open one of the compartments on a daily pill box. Instead of days of the week, each compartment was labeled with a different flavor of pot.

"Why so many different kinds?" I asked as Mike rolled the fattest joint I have ever seen, with one hand.

"Different strains for different pains, man," Jerry slurred.

"A few puffs of the Golden Goat," Mike popped Tuesday's slot, "you get a nice euphoric high that won't hinder your work."

"Gotta love the Goat," Jerry cheered.

"If you're looking to do nothing, a nice and potent indica like this Grape Ape here will have you locked to the couch for hours." Mike popped Friday's slot.

"Why the hell we talkin' 'bout the herb and not smokin' it?" Jerry chimed in.

"Fire it up, Jack." Mike handed me the joint.

"What kind was this?" I nervously asked.

"Moonlight Delight, it's an indica/sativa blend."

"You're the test pilot, Jack. It's gonna send you to the moon," Jerry howled just as I was about to spark the joint.

"Maybe I shouldn't." I let the flame die.

"You'll be fine; it's really mellow," Mike assured me. "I tried it yesterday."

"Thought you said we would burn the first joint together?" Jerry moaned.

"We are, but I had to burn a small bowl to make sure it cured properly."

"Yeah, yeah… Spark that shit up already, Jack." Jerry pouted.

I fired up that fat joint, took a big hit, and hacked my lungs out. Jerry burst with laughter and grabbed the joint.

"You been smokin' too much of Darla's sativa," Jerry laughed.

"You gotta cough to get off, right Jack?" Mike answered for me.

"Not me," Jerry said with a smoky voice as he held in his hit. He was just about to hand the joint to Mike when he exploded into a smoky coughing fit. The three of us burst into laughter.

"That's some tasty good shit, bro," Jerry hacked.

Our smoke swirled and danced and drifted high into the night sky until it faded into the hazy moon's blue. It really was a good high. I found myself jabbering about my past, to near strangers, like never before. Mike and Jerry listened to my tales of college woes and office work in cubicles with the fascination of savage natives hearing preposterous tales of modern life. I felt like I was accepted. I felt like I was already part of the family. And I felt like a complete idiot for believing Clancy's tales of the 'Campbell Clan of Psychopathic Killers.' I was completely ripped by the time Jerry was sucking the cherry right down to his fingertips. He sucked it twice more till the paper was nothing but ash blowing from his finger.

Christmas became a strange and blurry nightmare shortly after I stepped in off the deck. The beer, the booze, and the pot were not mixing well. My stomach was churning. The heat from the fireplace washed over me like a wave. I was dripping with sweat. I was going to puke at any moment. I ran for the bathroom. The door was locked. I was just about to turn and run for the front door when Darla snuck up behind me.

"Use my parents' bathroom," she whispered.

"You sure?"

"Yeah, it's at the top of the stairs, down the hall, on your left," is what I thought she said.

Nothing but moonbeams through the skylights lit the upstairs. I felt like I was intruding the moment I stepped off the stairs. My fingers fumbled along the wall with no luck finding a light switch. I kept my eyes to the floor and followed the wall until my fingers stumbled upon the last door on the left. The light switch was right inside the door. It looked like Easter when the lights shined: pinks, blues, greens, and pastels. Quilts and afghans, blankets and doily thingies were tacked to all the walls and draped over every piece of furniture. It was Betty's hobby room. Racks stacked full of fabric rolls, in every color, covered one whole wall. Another rack in the corner held a rainbow of strings and yarns. A giant quilt, swirled with blues and greens, covered the entire wall behind her sewing desk. I was just about to back out when I noticed a Blue Ribbon pinned to the bottom corner. I still don't know what made me walk over and read the ribbon: First Place Quilt Colorado State Fair, 1984. I stepped back to realize the quilt was an oddly distorted mosaic of the view of Lost Creek from their front window. It was a snowy mountain scene with a train rolling alongside the rippling river. Each little patch of color was no bigger than a scrabble tile — all sewn together to make a ten-feet-wide by eight-feet-high quilt. It was a work of art.

I stumbled around the room to realize all Betty's works were art. Even the afghan draped over the back of her desk chair looked like it should be hanging on the wall of some museum, swirled and marbled like an agate of blue and green. A dangling bundle of blue ribbons pinned to the wall next to the bookshelf was next to catch my attention. There must have been fifty blue ribbons, and not just for quilting and sewing, most of them were for her cooking. The bookshelf was full of cookbooks. I was afraid to touch many of them because they were so old they looked like they would crumble. One whole shelf was dedicated to notebooks, binders, and self-bound books full of handwritten recipes in perfect penmanship. They must have been passed down for generations. The pages were brittle and yellow. The recipes were strange. At the end of the row was a three-ring binder with a colorful crocheted cover. Inside, the recipes were different than the rest. They were handwritten like the others, but they were written out more like a play by play account. Every process was detailed: the time each took, the resulting look — "I cut the flour in and mixed the batter for ten minutes" — real boring stuff, I thought. There had to be at least forty recipes neatly slid behind the plastic sleeve of each page, all dated at the top.

I had flipped all the way to the back before I realized the backside sleeves weren't recipes — they were obituaries. The backside sleeve of every page held a newspaper clipping of the obituaries. The first obituaries were from the sixties; the last was from October 10, 2008: Mayor Kevin Connelly, 58 — died of sudden heart failure in his sleep… I turned back to the recipe side and skimmed through the ingredients — nothing out of the ordinary. The recipe was for snow goose in port wine sauce — porcini mushrooms were the only ingredient I suspected. Then I looked to the bottom of the page to see: Salad Preparation. It started off as your basic leafy salad tossed with the typical vegetables. "Three tomatoes on the Mayor's salad. Two on the rest," was the line that made the hair on the back of my neck stand straight. "Boil one-quarter cup of chokecherry roots for twenty minutes. Rinse the chokecherry roots and sprinkle only on the Mayor's salad. Sprinkle sprouts and almond slivers on all salads…"

Clancy was right. His drunken cackle roared through my mind like he was standing right next to me. Panic quickly set in. Visions of Sheriff Campbell storming into the room and blowing me away sent me running from the room.

I was pale as a ghost when I stumbled off the steps and into the great room. The Moonlight Delight had me so paranoid, I was sure Betty's hobby room had cameras. Everyone was staring at me. I was sure they had all just watched me find Betty's recipe book of death. I nearly jumped out of my skin when Darla snuck up from behind and pinched my ass.

"Thought you got lost," Darla said as I turned around.

"Lost? No… I was…"

"Are you feeling okay? You don't look so good."

"I don't feel so good."

Darla took me by the arm and escorted me straight to her house. She didn't even make me say goodbye to all her family. It was a cold and silent walk down the hill to Darla's. I ran straight for her bathroom, pretending I was going to be sick. I cranked the faucet for interference until the mirror was fogged over. "Go home," I quietly told my steamy reflection. That would be suspicious, my paranoid mind quickly countered. "Suspicious?" I laughed at my pathetic reflection. "I think we're past suspicious…"

Darla's phone rang to silence the voices in my head.

"Hello," her muffled voice answered over the running water.

I turned off the water just in time to hear Darla's tone turn concerned.

"Yeah, why? … Just a minute." The front door slammed.

Silence swept over the bathroom and the voices returned to chirp my certain demise: Did I put Betty's cookbook back on the shelf? You didn't. You dropped that thing and ran out like a little girl. I did… I had myself completely convinced that I didn't put the book back in its place. To this day, I honestly can't recall what I did with Betty's book. The silent chaos probably only lasted thirty seconds, but it felt like hours before the front door creaked opened.

"It's not a problem, Daddy." Darla's footsteps approached the bathroom door.

I didn't know whether she was still talking on the phone or if the sheriff was standing right outside the door ready to gun me down.

"Can you come out here?" Darla's sweet voice requested.

When I finally cracked the door to peek out, there was no one waiting on the other side to gun me down. Darla wasn't even there. I crept out to the kitchen to find her lying on the counter — completely naked — with a bottle of champagne. POP!

"Merry Christmas!" She grinned.

"Merry Christmas," I mumbled back.

"Everything okay?"

"I think that Honey Hop Ale and Mike's Moonlight Delight got the better of me."

"I know what'll make you feel better," Darla said with a wink, as she slid off the counter.

That's when I learned I have absolutely no willpower when it comes to women. One delicate little kiss on my neck and there was no resisting Darla's naked body pressed tight against me. I pictured everything around the kitchen to be a possible weapon for Darla to kill me as we kissed with a frenzy that bordered on violent. She ripped off my shirt so fast my head got stuck in the neck hole — I was sure Darla was going to bash my skull with the big cast-iron skillet hanging above the stove. She seemed furious as she yanked my pants off without even unbuckling my belt. But even the visions of her whipping out a knife and cutting it off while she was down there were not enough to make me run. Darla was a rage of energy and emotion that pulsed over me with every touch, tingling like warm spiders crawling across my every nerve. Looking back, I think it was the fear that made the affair so sensational. We threw each other around the kitchen with no regard. I thought I was going to explode after I slammed her into the stove and bent her over the burner, until I spotted her head pounding next to the knife block — the thought of Darla plunging the biggest of the blades deep into my belly kept me going. When she bucked me back, shoved me down on the breakfast bar, and climbed on, I was certain the scissors at the end of the bar would soon be stuck in my chest. Every position from kitchen to bedroom was surrounded by potential weapons for my certain demise.

The imminent sunrise was already washing golden over the pines as we fell to our backs. We were lying in puddles, gasping for breath, when we finally came to a twitching and quivering conclusion. My heart raced like never before. And the paranoia returned. I was certain some strange poison was already coursing through my veins, eating at the walls of my heart. All I could do was breathe deeply and twitch.

"What did you think of my family?" Darla rolled right back on top of me, her face just high enough to settle in the shadows, with her breasts beaming in the golden sunrise.

"They're great," I smiled, still staring at her perfect breasts.

"My dad didn't scare you?"

"No. We had a nice talk after the gift exchange game. Thank you, by the way."

"Of course. How about the food, it wasn't too hillbilly, was it?"

"Are you kidding? Your mom is a magician in the kitchen." My answer was drowning in regret the moment I said the word mom. It was as obvious to Darla as it was to me.

"You should see her cookbook collection."

I could feel her shadowy eyes glaring down at me, judging my response. "She collects cookbooks?" I answered in the guiltiest of voices. I didn't have to see her eyes to know she knew; I could feel the angry energy beaming from the shadows.

"We should get some sleep." Darla rolled over.

"Yeah, I'm beat."

It wasn't thirty seconds later that I heard Darla's nightstand drawer creak open. She had rolled over and reached for the drawer so quietly I almost didn't notice. But the slower she tried to pull on that drawer, the eerier the creak. And I pulled the covers over my face like a frightened child when she sprung back towards me.

"A couple puffs to help you to sleep?"

"No thanks," I finally answered when I peeked out to see it was only a joint she was pointing at my face.

"Looks like you could use it."

"I shouldn't."

"It'll help you fall asleep?"

"You wore me out plenty." I tried to turn on the charm. "I won't have any trouble falling asleep."

"Come on, don't make me smoke this thing all by myself." Darla was practically shoving the joint down my throat.

"Sorry, you're on your own." I expected to see Darla crush the joint and start screaming like a banshee before pulling a knife from under the pillow and jabbing it into my chest. Instead, she flicked her lighter to illuminate the sinister smile on her face, sparked the joint, and took three big hits.

"Your loss."

Darla was sound asleep before the smoke settled. And I was left wide awake to watch the sunrise burn color onto the valley until the little red numbers on Darla's digital clock ticked all the way to 9 a.m. That's when Darla yawned and rolled over. I pretended to sleep as she quietly climbed out of bed and tiptoed down the stairs. I ran straight for the bathroom. My reflection said I was already dead. My eyes were bloodshot red. My face was pasty. My head was dizzy and spinning. My throat was dry and swollen.

"Serves you right," I cursed my wretched reflection.
BANG! BANG! BANG! I nearly had a heart attack when Darla pounded on the bathroom door.

"Breakfast's ready," she said in the sweetest of voices.

"I'll be right down," I finally mumbled when my heart stopped shuddering.

The loft was swirling with the safe and happy aroma of cinnamon and sugar when I walked out of the bathroom. I stumbled down the stairs to find Darla bent over in front of the oven, wearing nothing but her apron, pulling out two big slices of her mother's apple pie. The crust was warm and crispy when she served it up to me at the kitchen table. My stomach was grumbling with hunger. But all I could think about was how to get out of there without eating Darla's pie.

"Do you not like it?" Darla asked as I poked at my slice, never taking a bite.

"I do, but my stomach's not too happy with me this morning."

"Coffee?"

"No, thanks."

"You wanna take a few runs?" Darla cleared my plate of mashed pie.

"I should really go home and feed Blue."

"Oh… okay." Darla's voice rang with rejection and anger.

"Tomorrow?"

"Yeah, tomorrow." Darla stormed off as I gathered my jacket and boots.

I was all geared up for my hike home, overheating, when Darla returned.

"See you tomorrow?" She surprised me with a kiss on the cheek.

"See you tomorrow." I reached for the door.

"A little something to settle your stomach?" Darla handed me a joint.

I spent that whole day in my shack, staring at that joint, waiting for Clancy to stop by. I didn't even take Blue for his daily hike. He grumbled and nudged me towards the door all day. Clancy never arrived. And I was glad he didn't. I had no idea what to say to him. How could I possibly explain to him the events leading to my finding Darla's mother's cookbook of death without admitting I had been sabotaging his investigation from the beginning? I considered telling him I had fallen for the enemy. I imagined Clancy's reaction to be unruly at best. By the time the sun set heavy on the west, I decided to play dumb and give the joint to Clancy as one last sample.

CHAPTER 7

The wind howled all night long. I didn't get a wink of sleep. I would have lain in bed all day if Blue hadn't been mumbling and groaning and nudging me out of bed as soon as the first signs of sunrise began to sparkle on the frosty window. Watching the sunrise from the porch in such a mood, with no joint to smoke, was much less spectacular than I had gotten used to. The pretty pinks burned red with sinister intentions. I waited, all morning, sure Clancy would show. He never arrived. By noon, I had to get out of the shack. Clearing my mind was a close second to Blue's pestering. As soon as I reached for my snowsuit, long before I strapped on the snow shoes, Blue was yipping and hollering, jumping and spinning around my feet.

The overnight winds had drifted the snow high over the trail. Step after fluffy white step was met with visions of the Campbell family jumping from the brush to ambush me. It wasn't until I had gotten almost to the river before the paranoia subsided. I had almost let the mountain serenity wash away my worries when the bush at my feet fluttered to life with such a commotion that my heart skipped a beat. Even Blue was startled. He wouldn't admit it, and he shook it off as soon as he saw I noticed, but he was scared — his eyes were the size of coke bottles. And a harmless little ptarmigan flapped high into the trees. All I could do was laugh, once my heart finally hit a regular beat.

I arrived at Clancy's shack without further incident. Smoke was rolling from his chimney — a good sign, I thought. But I still expected to walk in on the angry, drunken Clancy I had seen on Christmas Eve. I was pleasantly surprised. Clancy was cheery and chipper. He was sober. He still had a mess of papers scattered about the floor, but even they had a fresh new flow of organization to them.

"I was hoping you'd stop by," Clancy cheered as he ushered me in.

"Yeah, I thought I'd see you at my place yesterday."

"What was yesterday?"

"I thought you wanted to go to Boulder?"

"Boulder?" Clancy had no idea what I was talking about. He had no recollection of my Christmas Eve visit.

"Don't you want to have that pot tested?"

"What pot?"

"The pot I dropped off on Christmas Eve."

All the chipper cheer was flushed to white on Clancy's face.

"That was from Darla?" Clancy finally countered.

"Yeah…" I could tell from the look on his face that he had smoked it. My fear was further confirmed when I followed his hollow gaze to the empty bag on the kitchen table. "You didn't?" Clancy could only nod. And then he closed his eyes. Then he died. Not literally, but his spirit was dead. When his eyes finally reopened, it was clear as day. He had screwed up and he knew it.

"I thought that pot was from my old stash," he tried to sell the both of us. We both knew better. He didn't even remember finding it on the table.

The next hour was surreal, to say the least. A strange mix of acceptance and denial. One minute, Clancy was cursing this Earth and welcoming the unknown, the next, he was rustling through the research he had done on different poisons and denying all the symptoms. He was ready to leave this hard life and his sore body, but there were so many things he never accomplished.

And I knew, all the while, he hadn't been poisoned — well, I was fairly sure. Darla and I were on pretty good terms when I got the bag that bud came from. But I couldn't force myself to tell the truth. It was good for Clancy to come to terms, to evaluate his being — that's what I kept telling myself, anyway. But I really did think he would be better off — as long as he didn't have a heart attack from worrying about dying.

"How long ago did you smoke it?" I asked.

"I don't know… yesterday? The day before?"

"If it were poisoned, you'd be dead already."

"Not if it was ricin," Clancy waved a paper in the air. "That's one of her favorites… shit can take a week to kill you."

"Let me see that," I grabbed the paper. "Have you been nauseous?"

"No."

"You got the shits?"

"No."

"Been having seizures?"

"Not yet."

"You weren't poisoned by ricin."

Clancy was finally starting to come around when he realized he didn't have any of the symptoms. But I don't think he was convinced until I offered to smoke one of the roaches. And I was more than relieved when he told me not to.

"Yeah, I suppose we should save it to get tested," I replied.

"What's the point? I ain't dead."

"But this joint will surely kill you." I glowed as I pulled Darla's joint from my pocket.

"You got more?"

"Should we head down to Boulder tomorrow?" I asked, nodding my head, hopping Clancy wouldn't ask me why I was so certain the joint was poisoned.

"Thursday."

"Why wait till Thursday?"

"We have a meeting in Boulder."

"With who?"

"A young man Darla tried to kill."

"Who?"

"Chaz Saunders… Tracked his dumb ass down on Facebook."

"What!?"

"Didn't think us old farts knew about Facebook?" Clancy cackled. "Martin showed it to me at the library."

Clancy went on to tell me he had stumbled across his name when going through Martin's stack of *Nederland Gazette* criminal reports.

"I knew I heard his name before." Clancy's eyes lit up.

"What did he do?"

"DUI."

"Sheriff Campbell shoot him?" I joked.

"Don't go gettin' ahead of me, boy."

"Sorry."

"No, it wasn't till I came across his picture online."

"On Facebook?" I chuckled.

Clancy was not amused and his eyes alone told me not to interrupt again. "As I was saying… I remembered that goofy face right away. He rented old Milo Parker's place across from the Lost Creek Tavern fer a summer. Cocky sonofabitch, claimed to be some big rock star. Stupid shit had a taste fer the whiskey. Stupid shit couldn't handle it. Watched him get his ass kicked more than once outside the tavern. Still remember laughing with Martin when we heard he got his dumb ass pulled over by the State Patrol just after leaving the Wagon Wheel." Clancy paused for a long moment. From the glow in his eyes, I could almost picture the scene. "We were shootin' pool at the tavern when Gene came in with the news. That Martin could shoot a mean game. We used to play for hours, every Sunday in the summer, every Sunday he was around. I ever tell you 'bout his summer-long backpacking trips?"

"Yep," I answered, knowing Clancy would still repeat the story.

"Every summer he would find a new way to link different trails in a route that would lead him all the way to the Colorado border and back. Blue made a few of those trips." Clancy and I both looked over to see an excited look on Blue's face that let us know he knew exactly what we were saying. "Martin's previous dog, Powder, joined him fer at least ten of those summer trips. That Powder, she was an ornery bitch. A blue heeler like Blue, but that bitch was particular," Clancy chuckled. "She didn't like a single person aside from Martin. I knew that bitch fer over twelve years. Never once let me pet her. She'd a-never taken a liking to you like Blue…"

I had almost forgotten about Chaz by the time Clancy finally found his way back to the topic. He said Chaz was pulled over less than a mile from the Wagon Wheel. It was a Friday night, so he had to sit in jail over the weekend before going before the judge.

"Come Monday morning, he was foaming at the mouth and crapping his pants before the judge," Clancy cackled. "They say he died three times on the way to the hospital. It made the papers because Chaz came back and sued the county for the medical bills. The dumb shit thought he got food poisoning from the jail food.

"You wanna know why he lost?"

"Why?"

"Doctors said it wasn't food poisoning, said it was ricin, said the timing suggested he ingested the poison before he was arrested… Guess what the officer's report said was still burning in the ashtray when he pulled Chaz over?"

"What?"

"A big fat joint. Chaz swore he had just lit it, according to the officer's notes. That's why he swerved. He said he didn't even inhale. He just got it at the bar."

"So?"

"Who do you think he bought the joint from?"

"Who?"

"I'm betting on Darla."

"You haven't even talked to this guy?"

"That's what we're doing Thursday."

"You've arranged a meeting?"

"Not exactly… According to his Facebook page his band, Psychedelic Monkey, is playing at some bar down there. I Googled the address."

"So, you wanna drop in at the bar where his band is playing and ask him if he bought a joint from Darla… how many years ago?"

"Exactly, my boy." It made perfect sense to Clancy.

The sun was just about to set when I left Clancy's shack. The sky was grey and ominous. The wind was blowing sharp from the north, piercing my cheeks with icy crystals as I crunched through the snow towards the trail between our shacks. Branches cracked to warn of predators just out of view. I was in full sprint shortly after breaching the shadow of the tree cover. Blue thought it was a game and yipped and nipped at my heels all the way to my shack. I arrived just as the darkness settled into the valley for a long and cold night.

The first thing I did, after checking under the bed for Darla or the sheriff, was start a fire. Once the fire was roaring, I retreated to the safety of my covers. That's when the flickering fire brought the shadows to life. Strange silhouettes danced on the wall. I tried to hide my head under the covers, but not being able to see the scary shadows only amplified the eerie noises. The wind howled so loud it threatened to rip off the roof. My mind was racing. The visions turned more and more twisted and paranoid with every gust and creek. I was certain the Campbells were surrounding the shack. I could hear them outside, laughing and plotting. Blue was no help; he was sound asleep, snoring and whimpering and chasing in his dreams, two minutes after I lit the fire. Suddenly, I heard footsteps creaking on the porch and a strange rush washed over me. It was like nothing I had ever before felt. My heart raced faster than after Blue led me to the top of Lost Creek Peak. I couldn't breathe. My senses knew something my consciousness couldn't comprehend. So did Blue's. He sprung from his deep sleep with a full mohawk and a deep rumbling growl.

I slowly pulled Martin's rifle from under my bed and quietly slid the bolt back to feed a bullet into the chamber. I tiptoed to the window. It was far too frosty to see through. That's when that familiar creak of the top step cried over the wind. Blue was shaking with anticipation as I reached for the door. I got down on my knees, snugged the butt of the rifle tight to my shoulder and pointed it chest high at the door. I had barely turned the knob when Blue charged, bashing the door open with his head and roaring into the darkness. BANG! I accidentally jerked the trigger. Fire roared from the barrel to light the night like a flash of lightning just long enough to illuminate Blue sailing off the porch. The flash died just as I could make out the shadow of a coyote at the bottom of the steps. His tail was tucked so tight up his ass it was ahead of his nose. When my eyes were finally able to regain focus, all I could see was a swirling snow cloud around a rolling and tumbling, growling and yipping ball of chaos at the bottom of the steps. I don't think I had even comprehended what was going on when the commotion ended with a shrieking yelp. I thought Blue was dead. My instincts made me whistle. I think I thought the noise would startle the coyote into releasing Blue's throat. But I was quick to realize it was Blue that had the coyote by the throat. And Blue was just as quick to release the beast at the first sound of my whistle. I was quite surprised.

Blue was so proud. He had felt my panic. He had battled my fear. And he could sense my relief. He did a good job and he was honored to protect me. That's what his eyes said. And then the wind kicked up and the two touching aspens in the front yard began to rub and squeak, making me feel like a complete sissy for my visions of Darla and the sheriff laughing outside my shack. Even after such a realization, I still thought every sound was the sheriff. I tossed and turned for a good sleepless hour before grabbing the Jack London book and sparking the lantern. I was certain reading would put me right to sleep. I was wrong. There was no drifting off, that night. The book did do wonders for distracting me until my eyes got heavy, but the creepy outside noises always screamed as soon as I dropped the book.

I don't think I strung together more than an hour of sleep by sunrise. And I have never climbed out of bed so exhausted. But as tired as I was, I packed up my backpack and got Blue all revved up for a hike to Crater Lake. There was no way I was going to sit around the shack all day and wait for Darla or the sheriff to come by in search of my dead body.

The hike was just what I needed to take my mind away. The day was clear, bright, and blue when we left the shack. I had completely forgotten about the Campbells by the time we reached the tunnel. I was even laughing by the time we reached the first lake — at poor Blue swimming through the deep drifts. I figured we'd have lunch at the lake and then stop by Clancy's on the way back. The sun was still burning hot and bright when we reached the lake. I was way overdressed and a sweaty mess. We found a tall rocky cliff at lake's edge to eat lunch. With my legs dangling over the frozen-white lake, we watched a blizzard crest the Divide. The temperature dropped twenty degrees in two minutes. Snow was blowing sideways before I could finish my lunch. Blue circled nervously between my legs — it was time to go.

I was all bundled up and ready to head down the trail in no time. It was too late. We had barely found our way back to the trail before the heavy gray clouds turned the blue sky black. The snow was drifting so quickly our tracks coming up were completely blown over. I lost all sense of direction. But Blue seemed to know where he was going. I blindly followed him, even though I was sure he was leading us in the exact opposite direction. Four hours later, I knew I was never going to make it. We had made it down the mountain, but I had no idea which side. And trudging through that heavy snow, without the help of the downslope, was more than my trembling legs could handle. The air was so cold, and the snow was so wet, giant globs of heavy snow froze to the bottom of my snowshoes — it was like walking with concrete blocks on my feet. I could go no further. I tipped over in a drift to watch the flakes quickly cover me. My wet and sweaty clothes quickly froze crispy to my skin. I was ready to settle in.

I must have drifted off. I remember waking to Blue tugging at my pants. The thought of trudging through the snow kept me from getting up. But London's story, "To Build a Fire," about a man freezing to death on the Yukon Trail reminded me of one of Clancy's lessons: "If yer ever dumb enough to get yourself stuck in a blizzard, dig a snow cave." I heard Clancy's words and I dug a snow cave just like he had taught me. I dug the entrance low, opposite the wind. I dug it deep into a drift against the side of a hill. I made it just big enough for Blue and me.

My body had already warmed from the digging, so it was the serenity that I first enjoyed as I settled into my cave. The break from that persistent wind was heavenly. Everything calmed, and I thought for the first time in a few hours that I just might survive. But Blue would not join me. He just sat at the cave's entrance and whimpered. I tried to grab him and pull him in a couple times, but he wouldn't have it. And then he was gone, run off into the flurry haze and devoured by white. I couldn't believe that damn dog had ditched me. I was really counting on snuggling up to his furry warm coat. But there was just no way I could follow him. So, I put on every layer I had, plugged the entrance hole with my backpack, curled up in the fetal position, and drifted off to sleep.

"What in tarnation are you doing?" a gravelly voice rang through my dream. "Get on outta there."

My dark and peaceful cave was aglow with flickering yellow light when I opened my eyes. Once my eyes adjusted to the bright, I saw Clancy's angry face next to a flickering lantern in the entrance. I had dug my snow cave about thirty yards from his shack. Blue had barked outside Clancy's door until he followed Blue into the blizzard.

Clancy insisted I spend the night. I was not about to argue. And Clancy just so happened to have a big pot of rabbit stew on the stove.

"Got two nice ones just this morning," Clancy boasted as he served me up a bowl.

"Not supposed to kill rabbits this time of year," I whispered when Clancy turned his back.

"Pardon?"

"Smells wonderful." I replied, trying not to chuckle as I

remembered him telling me not take rabbits this time of year. I knew for a fact he had already killed at least twice what he said his yearly limit was. Anyway, the soup was absolutely delectable — as I imagine any meal so quick to follow certain death would be. And the security surrounding Clancy's company was absolute solace. He was in high spirits — rather than high on spirits. I think his "near-death" experience gave him a new appreciation for life.

"I ever tell you how I used to deliver ice to the Frozen Dead Guy?"

"Frozen Dead Guy? No."

"You'll get a kick outta this one," he cackled. "I met an old Norwegian lady named Aud at the Nederland market. It was 1993, I believe. She was an ornery old crow. A tough old bird. She and her son, Trygve, built a cryonics facility in a shed behind their house to keep Aud's father, Bredo, cryogenically frozen on dry ice…"

My eyes screamed with disbelief.

"True story," Clancy replied to my eyes.

"I didn't say anything," I answered back, like I actually believed him.

"She was somethin', that old bird." Clancy took a good moment to form her picture in his mind. "Even the way she said, 'Get away from me' drove me crazy — good crazy," Clancy winked at me through the orange glow of his fading fire. "I had to know everything about her. I spent the better part of two weeks in Ned, fending off the hippies bumming smokes, hoping to run into Aud. Finally, I spotted her posting a flyer. She was looking for a man with a truck. I told her she had her man. The job was to haul 1600 pounds of dry ice out to her property once a month. I did it all summer. Had to buy a truck," Clancy cackled. "Got an old seventies Ford pickup… good truck… only truck I ever owned. She's still out back, behind the still. Haven't started the old girl in years… not since Aud was evicted from her property back in '94 for living in a house with no electricity or plumbing. A violation of Nederland's new city ordinances. The city tried everything to get Aud's frozen father out of town. They even deported Trygve before '95 rolled around. In the end, the city officials were able to run Aud and her son out of town. But Bredo, the Frozen Dead Guy, still remains. My old friend Bo has been delivering dry ice to Bredo's shed since Aud left. It wasn't till after they put her on a plane that the city realized that the townsfolk enjoyed the myth surrounding the Frozen Dead Guy from Norway. She had barely landed when they decided to grandfather Bredo into the town. They even have a big Frozen Dead Guy festival every March. They make big money off him. And Aud still pays Bo to deliver dry ice to Bredo's shack, hoping to be able to return him to the cryogenics lab in Michigan where Bredo can finally rest in frozen peace.

"Why was it so important they keep him frozen?"

"Aud never told me. All she ever said was they wanted to keep him frozen until they could clone his cells. But I always got the feeling Bredo was some sort of royalty, or legend. It was Aud's only mission in life to make sure Bredo lived on."

I must have crashed shortly after that point. They next thing I remember is waking to the sound and smell of sizzling meat.

"'Bout time you got up. Thought I was gonna have to check yer pulse."

I stumbled over to the table just as Clancy was pulling his skillet from the fire.

"What is that?"

"Bambi bacon. Shot her while you was getting yer beauty sleep." Clancy pointed out the window at a deer hanging from the porch rafters. He had butchered a section of the hindquarters into thin slices that almost looked and tasted like bacon — if you haven't had real bacon in quite some time.

We were in my truck, rumbling down the hill for Boulder, before the "bambi bacon" settled. I was a mental wreck the whole way. No matter how I looked at it, I was an idiot. I had either fallen for a psychopathic serial killer, or I was dumb enough to believe the crazy tales of a crotchety old mountain man. Maybe Darla's mother was the only killer in the Campbell clan? I almost slid off more than a few Boulder Canyon curves pondering my predicament.

I was leaning towards believing Clancy when we dropped off the joint with Professor Kindberg. After some pressure from Clancy, he told us he could have the results in three days. We had to wander Boulder for six anxious hours before the dive that Chaz was playing finally opened. The place was a dingy little dive in a dark windowless basement on Pearle Street. The stage was nothing more than the floor in the corner — a few chairs blocked the instruments. We sat at the bar for almost two hours drinking stale beer before Chaz's band took the stage. They played four horrible songs, to an audience of three, before taking their first break. Chaz dropped the mic and stumbled straight to the bar. He was already drunk off his ass.

"Chaz, is that you?" Clancy asked.

"In the flesh, man. How you been?" Chaz asked like he knew Clancy, but his eyes said he had no idea who he was talking to.

"Still kickin' up in Lost Creek."

"Lost Creek? ... I love Lost Creek."

"Haven't seen you up there in some time," Clancy continued.

"That place nearly killed me, bro."

"I remember something about that. What happened?"

"Cops tried to poison me, man."

"That's right. Didn't you get pulled over in front of the Wagon Wheel?"

"Yeah, man. I just left the bar, barely sparked my J before the sirens were flashing in my rearview."

"So, they got you for smoking pot while driving?"

"Nah, man. I was drunk as shit, blew a .19. But that pig did confiscate my joint."

"You remember where you got it?"

"The joint?"

"Yeah."

"The bartender."

"Darla Campbell?"

"Yeah, man, Darla... I forgot all about her, man. What a body." Chaz stumbled off towards the stage in a daze.

Clancy was giddy as a schoolgirl as we left the bar.

"We got it, boy. The bitch is going down."

"Got what?"

"The smoking gun... or should I say joint," Clancy cackled.

"We don't even know for sure if she poisoned it."

"Not that joint. Chaz's joint. The one the trooper confiscated."

The drive up the hill was long, dark, and silent. Clancy was more convinced than ever. And that certainty in his eyes was really starting to freak me out. I would have rather fallen for Clancy's stories than Darla. It was nearly midnight when we arrived at Clancy's shack. After an hour of driving in the dark and thinking about what an idiot I had been, I convinced myself that the joint Darla gave me was poisoned. I didn't need to wait for three days.

Clancy's lantern was just starting to illuminate the room as I carried a bundle of firewood from the porch. Clancy was sparking a fire in the stove.

"We should call the cops." I dropped the bundle into the rusty metal wood bin next to the stove.

"Jesus crimany!" Clancy jumped back. "You tryin' to give an old man a heart attack?"

"Sorry."

"Cops... what cops we gonna call? Them boys in blue stick together. Sheriff Campbell finds out... we both know how that ends."

"So, what do we do?"

"Martin thought the newspapers were the best bet."

"Didn't someone already try that?"

Clancy had told me a story, back when he was first trying to convince me, about the suspicious shooting of Mary Jenkins, a twenty-three-year-old from California. She had followed her boyfriend, Bobby, a Lost Creek local and second cousin to Darla, back to Lost Creek. They rented the house right across from the Wagon Wheel. When winter came, Bobby's work ran dry and he started spending his afternoons at the Wagon Wheel. Mary always got an extra special beating the night after the unemployment check arrived. And it was one of those nights that Bobby beat her until both her eyes were swollen over. That was the night she finally called the cops. And she was shot dead in her doorway by Sheriff Campbell. The sheriff took some heat for that one. It seems a couple of tourists were stumbling out of the Wagon Wheel just as Campbell gunned her down. According to Campbell's statement: Mary was a raving lunatic and pointed a revolver at him. According to the two drunken witnesses: Mary was bleeding and crying for help when the sheriff drew down on her. There was a revolver bagged as evidence, but, according to a newspaper article in the *Nederland Gazette*, there wasn't a single fingerprint on the gun. In the end, Sheriff Campbell was cleared — according to the newspaper article — by a panel of his friends and family. The author, Randy Talbert, went berserk during the Frozen Dead Guy parade a few days after the article was published and ran through town wearing nothing but his cowboy boots and a coonskin hat, blasting his shotgun in the air until he finally blew his own head off in front of the Pioneer Inn. Clancy insisted Darla had drugged him.

"That didn't work out too well for Randy."
I think Clancy was taken aback that I had not only listened to his story but remembered.

"That's why we gotta go to the papers in Denver."

"You think anyone is going to believe the two of us?" I laughed, scratching my scruffy beard and looking over my tattered winter hand-me-downs.

"No one in their right mind," Clancy howled, as he beat clouds of dust from his crusty flannel. "That's why we need proof, my boy."

"The joint? … What if the tests come back negative?"

"The other joint."

"How do we get that if we can't go to the police?"

"We get the reporters to get it."

"And how do we do that?"

"We need to organize all Martin's evidence. Pick the most obvious cases and give them reporters so much they can't deny it. You take the sheriff. I've got a pretty good idea of what cases

I'm going to gather on Darla."

Clancy darted off to the closet and made laps back and forth dropping file box after file box on the floor before the fire.

"Definitely include the Mary Jenkins case," Clancy dropped a box at my feet. "Martin dedicated a whole box to her."

We stayed up the whole night. I never once even thought about being tired. The pine needle and pigweed tea Clancy brewed may have had something to do with that — it tasted like dirty socks sprayed with Pin Sol, but it kicked harder than a Red Bull.

"More vitamin C than a glass of orange juice," Clancy winced as he took a sip.

"Smells worse than your poop boots."

"Poop boots?!" Clancy roared with laughter.

"I can smell them sweaty old things from over here." I pointed to Clancy's old combat boots resting next to the door.

"Them boots is older than you, boy."

"I can smell."

"Well look who finally decided to grow a sense of humor."

Clancy and I kidded back and forth till the tea was gone. We both knew we were just procrastinating, but we also realized we had become true friends. We had reached that level where we no longer had to hold anything back — not that Clancy ever held anything back. The shack fell silent soon after, save for the crackling of the fire, as we turned our attention to our mission of organizing evidence.

Clancy crashed just as the sun freed the day critters from the clutch of the night's creatures. He was certain, just before drifting off, that even if the joint didn't come back poisoned he had gathered enough proof against Darla to send the reporters digging. And the morning's birds sang Clancy's victory song. I wasn't so certain.

I was even less certain about the evidence against Sheriff Campbell. Including Mary, Sheriff Campbell had killed nine people in the line of duty. The first three were in the first year he was sheriff — there wasn't much on those cases. Martin had gathered a stack of files on the last six. None of which proved that the sheriff was anything more than a quick trigger. All the shootings had been thoroughly investigated; the sheriff was cleared on every case. I knew he was guilty, but I knew about Betty's recipe book. And I toiled over that book all day. It was all the evidence we needed. I knew I should tell Clancy about the book. I knew he would be mad as hell at me for lying to him the entire time. But I knew he would come up with a plan to get it. Instead, I convinced myself such drama would only hinder our mission.

The following morning was Sunday. I arose with a mission. Lying awake all night, knowing we had no solid evidence and starting to doubt that Darla had actually poisoned that joint, I convinced myself that getting Betty's cookbook was the only option. I told Clancy I was going to take Blue for a walk. Blue was wiggly as a puppy the moment I said the word "walk." He was dropping a stick at my feet before I stepped off Clancy's porch. Fetching sticks in the deep snow was Blue's absolute favorite job. I say job because that was how Blue treated everything he did. Even play was a serious job that requires 100 percent at all times. The harder the job, the happier Blue was to do it. He loved when the stick sank deep into a drift. He would dive head first, with no regard for his safety, to retrieve it. He always brought the stick right back and dropped it at my feet. If I wasn't paying attention and walked past it more than twice, he picked it up and whacked me in the shin.

He was grumbling and whacking me in the shin the whole way to the highway. My mind was too focused to notice. The idiocy of my plan to break into Sheriff Campbell's home was very distracting. I knew it needed much more planning than a few half-asleep hours. But I knew I wouldn't have another chance for a week. The one thing I had learned about the Campbells, besides the fact that they were homicidal maniacs, was that they were strangely religious. Darla was always unavailable until at least two in the afternoon on Sundays. There was church from ten to eleven, a church social from eleven till noon, and then a Sunday brunch from noon till one or two. I figured I could get in and out shortly after Betty and the sheriff left for church.

Sheriff Campbell's house was surrounded by five acres of grassy valley — not a single tree for cover. Blue and I waded through the deep snow at the edge of the tree line on the north side of the property until we reached the ridge overlooking the backside of the sheriff's house. We had a perfect view of the sheriff's door as well as a clear line all the way down the highway until it dropped off towards Nederland — that's where the Campbells went to church.

Right on schedule, Betty and the Sheriff left for church at nine-thirty. They pulled out of the garage in the Sheriff's work truck, rumbled down their driveway, roared onto the highway, and dropped over the edge towards Ned. I waited in the cold drift for another twenty minutes — just in case they forgot something and had to return. It was right around ten when I tried the sheriff's front door. It was open just like Darla said it always was. Darla had told me the Campbells never worried about locking their door because no one would dare break into their houses.

I went straight for the bookshelf in Betty's hobby room. I was going to get in, grab the book, and get out. But the book wasn't there. Branches scratching at the window sent me screaming for the door. Blue roared like a mad dog and ran in circles like he was chasing ghosts. When he finally stopped and sat at my feet, he cocked his head and stared at me like I was some paranoid freak.

"Go watch the front door," I scolded, like he had done something wrong. Blue shook down his mohawk and scurried out with his tail between his legs. I felt horrible before he was out the door. I was just about to follow Blue when I spotted a footlocker that wasn't there on Christmas. The hasp was latched. I rummaged around the whole room and through every drawer for the key. It was nowhere to be found. I was just about to give up when I noticed a set of crocheting needles on the desk. Don't do it, I told myself as I jammed one of Betty's crocheting needles into the hasp. I didn't listen. The needle bent, but the hasp finally popped — nothing but sewing supplies inside. "Dumbass!" I scolded myself as I tried to bend the bent hasp back into shape. It was no use. "Now what are you going to do?" Get the hell out of here, my brain screamed.

I almost listened. I was down the hall and to the top of the stairs when I noticed a pink DARLA sign hanging on the door across from the stairs. I looked to the bottom of the steps to see Blue staring up at me, whimpering the same warning that was playing through my head — Don't go in. Again, I didn't listen. From the flowery pink sign on the door, I expected to walk into a world of fluffy pink pillows, unicorns, butterflies, and boy band posters — like she moved out at the age of twelve and her parents never changed a thing. It did look as if her parents hadn't touched it since she moved out, but the room was not at all what I expected. There were no stuffed animals, no pink bedspread, no boy band posters, no unicorns. It looked like a boy's room. The walls were plastered with posters, but they were of skiers and dirt bike racers. All the drawers of her desk were stacked to the top with old *Ski Magazines*. The bookshelf next to the desk was made entirely of old skis. And it was full of books. I remember thinking it strange she read so much as a kid. And such heavy books, both in size and content. I never read a single book growing up. None of my friends read books — or dared admit it. My parents didn't read. We watched television, movies on VHS, and played Nintendo.

I must have fingered through Darla's books for a good half-hour. I pulled book after book from the shelf and got angrier and angrier, realizing I hadn't heard of a single one. How could my parents have never introduced me to books? What would my life be like if they had? Then I spotted a familiar title: *White Fang* by Jack London. I recognized it because I had been looking forward to reading it for a few weeks. I finished the story before it, *The Call of the Wild*, not long after Clancy roped me into the Campbell conspiracy. I couldn't help but turn to the first page of *White Fang*. And *The Trail of the Meat* carried me far from Darla's bedroom. Grey Beaver had just given White Fang his name when the cuckoo clock in the great room took my attention from the book and alerted me to the fact that church was letting out. If the Campbells skipped Sunday brunch, they would be home in fifteen minutes. I shoved the book back on the shelf and started slamming Darla's desk drawers, thinking I could hide the fact that I was ever there, until I remembered they would know as soon as they found Betty's busted footlocker. I was just about to turn and run for the door when I noticed the shiny coil of a spiral-bound notebook at the very bottom of a pile of *Ski Magazine*s in the bottom drawer. The air turned electric. It seemed to draw my hand to that notebook like a magnet. The hair on the back of my neck was standing straight up when I read the balloon letters across the cover of the red notebook: Darla's Diary. All around the letters were pen-sketched snowflakes falling down the cover. I flipped to the first page to find Darla's first entry, written in perfect cursive:

Dear Diary,

Bradly Harper was a troll. He thought he was so much better than everybody else just because his parents were rich. All the money in the world and they'll never find their poor spoiled Bradly and his stupid leather jacket. I still can't believe he followed me out to Banger Mine. Boys are so stupid. After tormenting me for the last two years, he actually believed I was going to make out with him at Banger. The look on his stupid face when I jabbed my knife into his belly was priceless. I could have done without all the crying and begging. And all that blood, too messy. At least he had the decency to fall into the shaft…

Blue howled from downstairs to send me jumping to the ceiling. I ran to the window to see Sheriff Campbell's truck roaring up the hill. I crashed down the steps, bolted out the door, and ran for the woods. And I didn't stop until I reached the other side of the creek. I don't know of a single thought that went through my head from the moment I spotted the sheriff's truck till I was splashing through the cold creek. On the other side, all I could think about was the mess I left behind. Besides the broken lock on Betty's sewing locker, I'm pretty sure I left Darla's desk drawer open, as well as the front door.

I was a mental wreck when I stumbled through Clancy's door. Clancy could see it on my face.

"Yer pale as a kid just seen his mama naked," Clancy cackled as I kicked the snow from the treads of my boots. I didn't respond. "You alright?" All I could do was nod as I handed him Darla's notebook. Clancy's eyes lit up with a very different spark than mine had as his eyes trolled along the first few lines.

"Is this what I think it is?" Clancy drew the notebook to his chest and turned his eyes to the ceiling as if to give thanks to his Goddess of the Mountain. I was still nodding like a fool. "Where'd you get this?"

"I broke into her parents' house," I finally replied.

"You what!?"

"I found it in her old room."

"You broke in? … Like you broke a window, kicked down the door?"

"It was unlocked."

"So, they won't know you were there?"

"Uh…" I didn't have to continue. Clancy could see it in my eyes.

"What did you do?"

I went on to tell Clancy of the mess I left at the sheriff's house. Clancy was immediately on full alert. And the consequences of my actions were quickly realized as I watched Clancy pull an arsenal from under the floorboards beneath the kitchen table. I knew before he unzipped that big black canvas bag, after the unmistakable metal jangle as he dropped it on the table, that the bag was full of guns: handguns and rifles, and boxes and boxes of ammunition.

"You should have waited," Clancy growled as he jammed a clip into an old M14 and cocked the action. "We're gonna have the whole Campbell clan raining down on us."

"I'm sorry. I didn't think we had a case if the joint wasn't poisoned."

"Well, you should have waited to find out." Clancy threw a pack over his back, drew the rifle tight to his shoulder, and slid out the door. He didn't tell me where he was going or what I was supposed to do. And by the time I came to my senses and stepped to the door, he was long gone, just a straight snowshoe track heading west into the woods.

I turned to stoke the fire and worry. I knew, even if the Campbells were looking for me, they would never think to look for me at Clancy's. But that didn't stop me from sliding six bullets into Clancy's chrome .45 and pointing it at every creak and crack and squirrel scampering across the roof. By nightfall there was still no sign of Clancy. I was certain the Campbells had gotten him. That's when Blue began to grumble. I knew someone was coming long before I heard the crunchy footsteps stomping towards the door. I had that shiny barrel pointed straight at the door when Clancy blew in with the snow.

"You got the bees buzzing', boy," Clancy kicked the snow from his boots. He almost looked proud to see me pointing a gun straight at his head.

"Sorry." I quickly dropped it.

"Don't be. You started a war this afternoon."

"A war?"

"Every Campbell within a hundred miles is in town. They've already got two riflemen on your shack."

"Riflemen?"

"I was pissed to beat hell at you, boy, until I called Kindberg." Clancy shook his finger at me. "You were right... the joint wasn't poisoned."

The smile on Clancy's face told me I should be happy, but all I could think about was the fact that Darla hadn't tried to kill me. Something from some deep dark pit in my gut was trying to vindicate Darla's homicidal nature. For all I knew, everyone she killed deserved it. Even Martin: just because Clancy said a few good words about him didn't mean he wasn't a bad guy.

"We're gonna have to sleep in shifts," Clancy interrupted my thoughts as he threw a log into the stove.

"You think they're going to come here?"

"If they're smart."

"Why?"

"There's a highway of tracks between our shacks."

I hadn't thought of that. We took turns, in two-hour intervals, watching the darkness. I conveyed my concerns of not being able to tell if anyone was approaching, but Clancy quickly assured me that I would know.

"If the night turns a fiery red, we got company," Clancy chuckled, as he set the kitchen chair in front of the window. He had surrounded the whole perimeter with trip wires that would ignite flares if anyone tripped them. "Get some sleep. I'll take first watch."

I didn't get a second of sleep. I was dead tired and staring at the ceiling when Clancy shook me out of bed for my first watch. He was sawing logs five minutes later. And, now that I had to stay awake, I could hardly keep my eyes open. I couldn't keep my mind off Darla's diary.

I turned to her second entry, hoping to find some sort of evidence to explain how the Darla I knew could be the monster of her diary, hoping to learn that her parents had somehow brainwashed her into such behavior. Her second entry did anything but:

Dear Diary,

I really screwed this one up. I stabbed Amy Walters at last night's jubilee camp-out. Daddy's so mad at me. I don't know why they had to put us in the same tent. She just wouldn't shut up about kissing Johnny at the Fourth of July fireworks. She knew we were still dating on the Fourth. She was rubbing it in my face. So, I jammed a tent stake in hers. I stuck her right in her big fat mouth. She was so surprised. For the first time ever, she couldn't say a word. She tried to scream, but she could only gurgle as the blood puddled in her throat. Then she erupted like a volcano, spewing red-hot blood from her mouth before falling back onto her pillow. I knew she was going to die. I could see it in her eyes. And I still stabbed her in the chest another fifty times. Amy was peppered with oozing red holes when I rolled over, killed the lantern, and fell fast asleep as her warm blood flooded across the nylon floor of the tent. I didn't even remember what I had done as I woke with the sun, until that sticky red mess reminded me. I could hear Daddy and the other chaperones rustling around to get a fire going. I knew they would be waking us up at any minute. That's when my instincts took over. Daddy always told me to listen to them in such situations. 'The voice of preservation,' he calls it. He says he has the same voice, only us special people have it. The voice told me to pull the tent stake from Amy's chest, rip a hole in the back of the tent, and then hide the stake in my backpack. Then the voice told me to scream. I screamed bloody murder. Daddy was the first into my tent. I could see in his eyes he knew what I had done. 'Get the rifles,' he yelled to the other chaperones. 'Don't move,' he said before storming out. I didn't know what to think until I heard Daddy yelling about coyotes attacking the campsite. He sent the chaperones out to kill the rabid beasts. I thought I was in the clear, until I saw the look on Daddy's face when he stormed back into my tent. I could see the anger in his eyes, but it was the disappointment that really hurt. He made me tear every one of the puncture wounds to Amy's chest, so it looked like she was ripped apart by teeth and claws. I didn't think it was a punishment, until I started. I thought I would enjoy shredding that bitch. But knowing she was long dead and feeling nothing, it was just gross. The coroner didn't give a second look and agreed with Daddy and concluded it was the work of a pack of coyotes. But that didn't stop Daddy from giving me a dozen licks with his switch the moment we got home. At least Mom understood.

I was wide-awake after that entry. And I was sure I heard the Campbells closing in on Clancy's shack for the rest of the night. There was no way I was sleeping, even during Clancy's watch. The sun finally rose before any of Clancy's alarms blazed.

CHAPTER 8

The light was still gray when we snuck out of Clancy's shack. Our mission was to hike into town, so Clancy could set up a meeting with a journalist that Professor Kindberg knew. We followed the river all the way to where the valley opens before town. We climbed the ridge to the south for a view of the entire town. It was buzzing with the angry relatives of Sheriff Campbell. Clancy left Blue and me on the ridge to try to make it to the payphone alone. I watched his blurry figure cross the highway and approach the phone booth on the north side of the Wagon Wheel without notice. The mob of Campbells was swarming on the south side. He was only in there for about two minutes, but it felt like a lifetime.

Clancy returned without notice. We were set to meet Barry Parker from the *Denver Post* in Black Hawk. We had four hours to get there and Sheriff Campbell's riflemen were still sitting on my shack. Clancy pointed them out from the cliff across the river from my property. There was no way we were sneaking my truck out. Not that we'd ever make it through Lost Creek if we did.

"We could hitchhike," I suggested as we approached Clancy's shack.

"Shush!" Clancy whispered, raising a finger to his angry

mouth.

We circled all the way around to the back of the property, stopping every ten steps to listen. We wasted almost an hour tiptoeing to Clancy's shack. When we were finally close enough to see it, Clancy handed me his rifle.

"Shoot anything that moves," Clancy cocked a black .9mm, "anything that isn't me." He was on the ground and army-crawling toward his shack before I had a chance to respond, slithering like a salamander through the snow faster than I'd ever seen him walk. Getting back to his feet once he reached the shack was another story; he looked more like a turtle stuck on his back as he pulled himself up the railing of the porch steps. He crept one circle around the shack and then waved me over.

We only had three hours to get to Black Hawk. We had no ideas on how to get there. I thought we should try to get Clancy's old truck running. He said she would fire right up. But even if she had gas and we could get her dug out in time, Clancy was certain we wouldn't make it to the highway before the Campbells gunned us down.

"You know anything about snow machines?" Clancy lit up.

"Snow machines… like a snowmobile?"

"Whatever."

"Yeah, I drove 'em all over as a kid."

"You fix 'em?"

"I'm terrible with engines."

"Figures."

"Why?" I asked, seeing the wheels in Clancy's mind were too busy turning to answer.

"You got gas in yer truck?" He finally snapped out of it.

"Half tank, I suppose."

Clancy jumped up and grabbed his coat. "Wait here."

"Where are you going?"

"Get gas."

"For what?"

"We're gonna 'snowmobile' to Black Hawk."

"You have a snowmobile?"

"Hasn't run in years, but I should be able to get her to turn over without too much work."

"Let me get the gas."

"What the hell do you know about sneaking into the cover of enemy fire?"

"I can do it."

"How would you approach?"

"From the west," I blurted out without giving it any thought. "The guy at the end of the driveway can only see to the front porch at best. The guy watching the door and the back of the property will never see me if I come out of the trees at the back-west corner." I could see the approval brewing in Clancy's eyes and I knew I was saying all the right things, even if I had no idea where they were coming from.

Ten minutes later, I was stomping through waist-deep snow with no snowshoes — they were far too noisy. I was all the way to the river, swinging a wide loop around my shack to make sure no one heard me, when I looked back to see Blue tunneling through the snow behind me. I had told him not to follow. He knew exactly what I was saying. And then he waited until he knew I couldn't make a sound to catch me. My eyes screamed, Bad Dog, as he parted the drift at my feet. He knew exactly what my eyes said, and he went all wiggly and licked my face because he knew it worked every time. I shook my finger at him one more time before continuing on, with Blue on my tail.

We were crouched in the snow behind the trees to the west of my shack when I realized it would probably be the heavy stench of spray paint that gave me away. Clancy insisted I not only paint the red gas can white, but also my brand-new ski suit — I still believe he only made me do it because he thought it was too new and fancy. Anyway, my nice new ski suit was spattered and stinky with crusty white paint. Blue was frozen over and matted with snow, so he was also well camouflaged. We tunneled through the snow to the shack with no problem. I peeked around the east corner to see the second guard was still in the same position. I had a clear line, straight to the truck.

"Stay," I whispered to Blue. Between the quiet angst in my voice and the serious dread in my eyes, Blue got the message.

I had never siphoned gas from a car. But with Clancy's detailed instructions, I had the fuel flowing after only swallowing a small amount. Everything was going exactly to that strange plan I don't ever remember conceiving. When the can was half full — Clancy said that was all we would need and I shouldn't try to carry any more — I slowly and silently slid the hose out of the truck. I quietly screwed on the gas cap. Then I slowly closed the little door, forgetting about that wretched SCREECH that always followed.

"Bobby! We gots company!" A rifle blasted.

I could hear Bobby stomping and huffing up the driveway.

"Where's he at, Daryl?" Bobby gasped as he stopped to catch his breath no more than twenty yards from the front of the truck. Daryl didn't answer, but I could tell they were somehow communicating. The silence was quickly broken by the slow crunching of footsteps coming my way on both sides of the truck. I pulled Clancy's .9mm from my pocket, hearing Clancy's voice, "You sure you know how to use that thing?" I said I did. I didn't have a clue. But even worse than not knowing whether I had just flipped the safety on or off was the uncertainty about being able to pull the trigger if I had to. I had shimmied around to the back of the truck just before Bobby stepped into view. They were slowly marching towards me. I thought about running for the trees, but the visions of being shot in the back were too overwhelming. Should I throw my hands in the air and give up? Even though I knew that last option would still surely end in death, the possible extension of life was very appealing. That's when Blue went rabid and charged Bobby with his screeching rumble. Bobby nearly blew off his own foot he was so startled. Blue bounded through the snow and got all the way to the path up the driveway before Daryl and Bobby realized what was going on and started shooting. I jumped up, grabbed the can of gas, and ran for the cover of the trees on the south side of the lot. I was sure they had turned around to see me and were firing straight at my back as I dove over the drift where the aspens got thick. I peeked back over the drift to see they still had their backs to me.

I escaped unnoticed. And all I could think about was Blue. I lugged that heavy gas can all the way to Clancy's shack telling myself there was no way they could have hit him — he's too fast. So fast he should have circled around by now, I reminded myself. I decided I would deliver the gas to Clancy and then go back for Blue.

"God damn carburetor!" Clancy cried, before dropping his wrench and reaching for his rifle when I approached his shed. That's when Blue came yipping up the path. It was such an awkward whine I was sure he had been hit. Then he leaped through the air and tackled me into the snowdrift to lick my face like a little puppy.

"Took you long enough," Clancy grumbled as he grabbed the gas can.

I could only smile. And it wasn't just from Blue's kisses or the bliss of knowing he hadn't been hit. I had just done something real for the first time. I was alive, for the first time. I'm afraid I will crave that fighting-for-your-life feeling for the rest of my days.

It was such a rush I almost didn't notice the relic of a "snow machine" Clancy was working on. It was a 1976 John Deere Cyclone 440, bright green with rainbow stripes. The windshield was jagged and broken. The black leather seat was tattered, and mice had long ago absconded with the foam padding to insulate their nests. I just risked my life to get gas for this pile of shit? I was certain Clancy wouldn't get that thing running even before I looked under the hood to see he had the whole motor torn apart.

"Are you serious?"

"You're in my light," Clancy grumbled before hammering at the engine with his wrench.

"You really think you can get this thing running?"

Clancy ripped something off the engine that looked important. Tubes and wires dangled with no connection.

"How 'bout you make yourself useful and pack everything to show the reporter in yer backpack?" Clancy's raspy tone suggested he was in no mood for banter.

I shuffled off to the shack without another word. Even Blue knew to tuck his tail and follow.

We were down to an hour as I stepped onto Clancy's porch with my heavy pack on my back. Clancy was just dropping the hood when I approached the shed. The rusty hinges broke and the hood crashed to the ground.

"Don't you say a word." Clancy shook his finger at me. I said nothing as he straddled the seat, flipped the choke, jammed the throttle, and yanked the rope three times. The poor old snowmobile shuddered and blew black smoke.

"Three pulls with the choke on," he instructed before flipping off the choke. "And then one more pull." He yanked the rope and jammed the throttle. That old John Deere rumbled and coughed blue smoke. BANG! It backfired and I dropped to the ground, as if I'd been shot. Clancy laughed his ass off. He was still laughing when he dove for the engine with a screwdriver as it started to sputter. Suddenly, that old John Deere was roaring like a champ. Clancy heaved the hood over the engine, latched it down on each side, and then hammered on the front of the hood with his wrench until he smashed a hole through the fiberglass. I thought he had gone berserk, until I saw him threading a rope through the hole and tying the hood to the front bumper where the rusty hinges had failed. I was still in shock that the relic had actually started when Clancy climbed aboard and jammed the throttle. The old John Deere howled as it raced across the beaten snow around the shed. Then it gurgled and nearly drowned as Clancy dove into the deep snow and raced a test circle around the shack. He had barely skidded to a stop before he was frantically waving me over.

"Let's go!" he scolded.

I threw my leg over the tattered seat, sat on the hard metal tunnel, and quickly looked for something to hold. I found where the passenger's handles were supposed to be; they were both broken off long ago. I was just about to settle for wrapping my arms around Clancy's waist when he jammed the throttle. My legs were up and over my head and my ass was in the snow before I knew what had happened. Clancy had no idea and buzzed off into the deep white. Blue's bark scolded me for doing something so stupid as I picked myself out of the snow. Clancy made it all the way to the river before I heard that poor John Deere throttle down and turn around to come back for me.

"We ain't got time fer games, boy," Clancy cursed, as the snowmobile slid to a stop.

"Let me get a grip before you take off."

Blue was yipping and tugging at my pant leg when I climbed on.

"Knock it off, Blue."

Blue stopped and sat, staring intensely at the track, waiting for it to make its move. Clancy jammed the throttle the moment I wrapped my arms around his waist. And Blue was barking and biting at the track the moment we took off.

"No, Blue! You stay... Bad dog!"

Blue stopped in his tracks the moment the words "bad dog" left my lips. Even though I couldn't see Blue's woeful eyes through the dusty snow spraying up past the half-gone mud flap behind us, I could feel them burning on my back. "You're a good boy, Blue," I said as if he could hear me over the whining John Deere. "You're the best dog in the whole world." I looked back to see Blue sitting, perfect as a statue, as we dropped over the hill before the river.

We only had forty-five minutes to make it to Black Hawk. It took us ten minutes just to cross the river. That proved to be the easy bit. The trail turned upward on the other side. There wasn't a single track to follow. Clancy was unabashed. We climbed much higher than I expected before the Cyclone's track was buried and spinning in place — about twenty yards. It took us ten minutes to get dug out and moving again. We were buried a minute later. We practically had to walk that damn Cyclone up the side of the mountain after that. Clancy pushed from the side as he held the throttle and guided the steering; I pushed from the rear. The sun was already setting over the Divide as we pushed the Cyclone to the top of the ridge. It was a spectacular view. To the east, the city lights were just beginning to twinkle. The sun was burning red on the West. But we had no time to regard it. It was all downhill from there.

Clancy pegged the throttle the moment the Cyclone was pointed downhill on a clear path. With the help of gravity we were swimming down the side of the mountain. The deep resistant snow was now our friend and we floated on a pillow of white. Aside from sliding sideways into a few trees, we made it down the mountainside without incident. But the sun had descended below the trees and the Cyclone's headlight had burnt out years ago. We launched off drifts without ever seeing them — I was certain the suspension would fail. We bounced off rocks — I expected the skis to be ripped off at any moment. We launched off a snowplow berm in the Gilpin County School parking lot and sailed right over Peak to Peak Highway. The snow was not soft and pillowy on the other side. The Cyclone's shocks buckled as we crashed down on the windblown snow of Missouri Lake. A wretched ratcheting was banging under my seat. The track treads were thumping the undercarriage. Clancy was unrelenting, and he pushed the Cyclone on.

The engine finally exploded in the middle of a snowy meadow. Flames roared from the vents right above Clancy's feet. He dove off with me still holding tight to his waist. The poor Cyclone torpedoed into a drift. All but the flickering taillight was buried, with the flames melting the hood and glowing orange through a foot of translucent snow. The glow got brighter and brighter as the snow ceiling melted. I was secretly glad it burst into flames. I was freezing on the back of that thing. Well, I thought I was freezing, until I picked myself out of the drift to feel the stinging cold of melting snow dripping down my neck — now, that's freezing. I waded straight through the deep white to huddle over the wreckage and absorb the warm glow.

"Wouldn't do that, if I was you," Clancy warned before cursing and kicking at the snow; the flames had melted his boots and the bottoms of his snow pants were still smoldering.

"Why's that?"

"Soon's them flames melt the gas line… BOOM — you ain't gonna be cold no more."

"I don't care," I mumbled. I really didn't. I was so cold.

The sky was clear and black. The Big Dipper was shining bright and laughing at me as it pointed to the North Star. And the frigid north wind was peppering my frosty cheeks with icy shards. The flames quickly burned a chimney through the drift. The flickering orange glow was so warming — for about thirty seconds. Then the snowy ceiling above the fire collapsed and the orange glow died with one quick and steamy sizzle.

"We'll be as dead as that fire if we don't get movin'," Clancy insisted.

I was done. The last thing I cared about was whether or not we were going to make it to meet the reporter. But I knew Clancy was right; we would never survive the night in that frozen meadow. It took everything I had to get me walking on my frozen toes. They were long past the point of cold; tingly and numb would have been a welcome sensation. Ten hard steps from the wreckage, the cold was long gone. The snow was waist-deep and the toil turned me sweaty and stripping layers before we reached the relief of the trees. The walking became much easier under the cover of the trees. The canopy had only allowed about two feet of the heavy white to pile at its feet. We followed a nicely packed game trail to the edge of the forest. Straight below us was Black Hawk, about a thousand feet straight down a rocky cliff. It was much too steep to climb.

"There's an old mining road just up the way that leads down to the road," Clancy assured.

Sirens screamed the moment we set foot on the pavement. They were coming from up the hill, from the direction of Lost Creek. Flashing red and white lights were quickly approaching. Clancy raced across the highway and dove over the shoulder. I followed with no thought. The astonishment in Clancy's eyes quickly told me my worries were just. He was certain, as was I, that the sheriff had somehow tracked us to that very point. We were buried deep in the snowy brush by the time we realized it was only an ambulance. The relief shone bright on Clancy's face. The reprieve from such certain fate was energizing. We pulled ourselves out of the ditch and trudged along the slushy shoulder with renewed fervor.

The crowd was electric and buzzing with dreams of striking it rich when we finally stumbled upon Main Street. It almost felt like we were on the right path, like we were supposed to be there at that very moment, like the energies of the earth had somehow drawn us to that very setting. It was destiny. We were fifteen minutes late, but it felt as if we were meant to be. We would have ended up at the front door of the Fitzgerald, at that exact moment, even if I had never moved to Colorado. I rode that strange wave of ordained energy right through the front doors and across the casino floor. I noticed nothing as I followed Clancy to the bar where we were supposed to meet Barry Parker.

"He said he'd be wearing a black jacket and an orange stocking cap," Clancy mumbled.

"How old is he," I questioned, looking over the crowd of seniors at the bar.

"Yer age."

There was no one wearing a black jacket and orange stocking cap. There were no more than a couple people anywhere near my age, none that looked like reporters.

"That hack bastard!" Clancy cursed.

"Maybe he's running late," I offered with little conviction.

"He ain't late; he ain't comin'."

Something in Clancy's voice told me he knew something that I didn't. And the friendly energy that had carried me in was instantly sucked away and the noise of the casino suddenly flooded my perception, laughing ominous chants. The crowd went from mute to max in a blink of an eye. The slots suddenly dinged with impending doom. And the realization that Barry Parker had never intended on meeting us quickly crossed my mind. I imagined the phone conversation between Clancy and Barry — Barry was laughing his ass off as he hung up the phone after listening to a crazed Clancy grumble his preposterous tale. Our frozen trip was bound to be fruitless.

"How long we gonna wait?" I asked as I leaned into the corner and took off my wet jacket.

"Don't be getting' too comfy."

"Why's that?"

"They know we're here."

"Who does?" I knew the answer before I saw the "you dumbass" look on Clancy's face.

"You see that guy standing at the front door pretending to read the paper?"

"Yeah."

"Don't stare!" Clancy swatted me in the back of the head.

"I wasn't," I cried.

"He's been there since we walked in."

"He could be security?"

"He ain't security."

"How could the Campbells possibly know we're here?"

"How the hell should I know?"

"What should we do?"

"Look fer a way out of here."

Clancy's eyes darted about the crowd like a paranoid junkie; his intensity was unsettling. My attention was attracted by a woman's nasally voice, "Sorry I'm late, Stan." I couldn't see where the voice was coming from, but it was so annoying, it was all I could hear. It was soon apparent she was the nightshift bartender. She was late relieving Stan. She swore up and down that it wasn't her fault. There was a car accident in Gregory Gulch. Someone sailed over the edge. She saw the paramedics hauling a dead body out of the river as she drove past. Traffic was backed up all the way to Golden.

"There was a car accident," I blurted.

Clancy responded with a hostile eye.

"Maybe he's just late," I continued.

"Maybe he's the one dead in the river." Clancy had also heard the bartender's remarks. His reply was meant to disparage, but the moment he said it we both knew it was true. We didn't need to read the morning paper to know that it was Barry Parker that went sailing over the edge.

The happy gambling faces glared with sinister intentions. The dinging slots were ringing like a thousand angry alarm clocks — Wake up! My attention immediately turned to the man at the door. He was still standing in the same spot, pretending to read the same page of the paper. I couldn't make out his face, but there was something eerily familiar about his cowboy hat. It was a big thing, a ten-gallon kind of thing. And that's when it hit me; I knew that hat. That was Darla's brother's hat. That was Bill. The Campbell family Christmas suddenly flooded my memory. His wife gave him that hat for Christmas. "It's a Stetson, just like the one Buffalo Bill wore." I heard Bill's scruffy voice like it was Christmas.

"He's a Campbell," I whispered to Clancy.

"No shit, Sherlock… There's two more at the other door."

"What do we do?"

"Follow me."

Clancy trotted off like nothing was bothering him. I followed, but with more of a paranoid Frankenstein step, constantly surveying the casino to make sure no one was rushing in on us.

"How 'bout a drink, darlin'." Clancy's flirtatious tone turned me around just in time to trip over the bar stool and nearly face-plant into the bartender's impressive cleavage. With everything that had been going on, I had failed to notice the ridiculously revealing uniforms of the staff, tight little black dress things cut to look like a tuxedo jacket on top.

"What's your poison?" It was the nasally lady. The nametag pinned to her lapel read Peggy. She was leaning over the bar, strangely close to Clancy. Peggy had to be pushing fifty, but you could tell she took great care to hide it. Her thick black curly hair was as big as Dolly Parton's — I think her breasts were bigger.

"How 'bout two fingers of yer best whiskey?" Clancy answered.

"Coming right up."

"Are you kidding me?" I turned to Clancy to see him drooling over the sight of the bartender bending over to grab his bottle.

"Thank you, darlin'." Clancy tipped his hat as she slid the whiskey to his awaiting hand.

"What can I get for you?" She turned to me.

"The boy ain't drinking," Clancy answered.

"Good idea to have a designated driver in this town."

"Designated driver! Ha! He can't drive fer shit when he's sober." Clancy leaned close to Peggy. "But he counts cards like a sonofabitch," he whispered. "Don't cha, my little Rain Man?" Clancy turned to me and ruffled my hair like I was six.

"You're funny," Peggy giggled, as she brushed her hand along Clancy's dirty leather sleeve.

"I don't really count cards," I cut in.

"Don't lie, boy. Peggy don't care if you count cards. Do ya darlin'?"

"Not if you cut me in," she kidded.

"Oh, I'll cut you in, alright," Clancy smirked. "How 'bout after me and the boy take twenty er thirty thousand off the casino you and me go get some steak and lobster?"

"I'm allergic to seafood."

"I suppose next yer gonna tell me you don't eat meat?"

"I love red meat."

"Oh, really?" Clancy jabbed me with his elbow. "I 'er tell you I was half Indian?" Clancy cackled.

Clancy continued on like he was Rico Suavé. Just hearing the steamy banter between Peggy and Clancy was more than enough to turn my stomach. Even more disconcerting, she was eating it up. She was leaning over the bar, intently listening to Clancy's crap, totally flirting. I had no idea what was going on. One minute he tells me the Campbells have the casino surrounded and we are moments away from being dragged off and executed by Sheriff Campbell; the next, he's trying to score a date with the big-breasted bartender like we were on vacation. I thought I had lost my mind. Suddenly, the casino's noise roared over Clancy's banter. Dinging. Ringing. Yelling. Screaming. The crowd. The vicious, roaring crowd. I was convinced I had lost it when my mind was once again able to filter out enough of the noise and chaos to comprehend Clancy's conversation.

"You saw the body? That's horrible," Clancy condoled. "You just never know."

"You never know," Peggy moaned.

"It really makes a guy think."

"Sure does."

"So, Peggy, what would you do if you knew tonight was your last night on earth?" Clancy asked with a wink.

"You're naughty," Peggy giggled, sensing the same bullshit that had me rolling my eyes. What neither of us realized was that Clancy's angle, though cunning, was not of the perverse nature we assumed.

"You have no idea, darlin'... But seriously, I've been trying to answer that very question for myself ever since I ran into that gentleman over there in the entryway." Clancy pointed to Bill.

"That guy reading the paper?" Peggy asked with genuine concern.

"That's the one."

"What'd he do?"

"Ah, he didn't do anything, just somethin' he said."

"What'd he say?"

"Oh, I don't want to worry you... he's just some crazy tryin' to get a rise outta people."

"What'd he say?"

"He said I was 'going to burn in hell if I stepped foot in this cesspool of sin.'"

"Oh..." Peggy breathed a sigh of relief.

"I know, pretty humdrum... guess it don't take much to get an old guy like me thinkin' 'bout dyin'... Like that wacko would actually blow the joint up."

It must have taken thirty silent seconds before Clancy's words penetrated Peggy's brain.

"He said he was going to blow up the casino?" Peggy was shaken.

"I didn't mean to startle ya, darlin'. He ain't gonna blow nothin' up. He's just a nut."

Peggy said nothing as she stared at Bill with a genuine fear in her eyes.

"Suppose we should do a bit of gambling?" Clancy turned to me with a smirk.

"Okay?"

"What do I owe ya, darlin'?" Clancy polished off his whiskey.

"It's on me," Peggy muttered.

"For your pleasantries," Clancy tossed a ten on the bar and trotted off.

Peggy stood like a statue, staring at Bill with her mouth wide open, as Clancy disappeared into the crowd around the slot machines. When I finally rushed off to catch him, Peggy ran for the bright red phone on the wall behind the bar. She was frantic as a peacock. I couldn't hear what she was saying, even though she was practically screaming into the receiver. I found Clancy sitting at a slot machine about thirty yards from the bar.

"She's calling security," I blurted as I sat at the neighboring machine.

"About time."

"How 'bout we think about how the hell we're going to get out of here?"

"That's the plan."

"You think you could share?"

"Jesus, kid, you been payin' any attention since 9/11?"

"What the hell does 9/11 have to do with this?"

"The whole world's paranoid. Even the smallest of communities believe terrorists are plotting to bomb their town."

"So?"

"So, there's no better security than that of a casino."

Clancy fed a dollar into the slot, pulled the handle, and spun around on the swiveling seat like his move was choreographed. His eyes dared me to turn and see the production he had set in motion. All I had to do was follow his gaze to realize that he had planned the whole debacle from the moment he stepped up to big-breasted Peggy. It led me straight to the vision of three black-suited thugs swarming upon Bill. But Clancy didn't move until he spotted three other "spies" rushing to Bill's aid.

"Time to go." Clancy jumped from his stool and tugged at my arm.

The commotion was enough to let us out the door without notice. We hit the sidewalk in full sprint. Well, as full a sprint as Clancy could manage. I was constantly slowing to a stop to wait for Clancy's hobbling old ass. That's when I noticed two

Campbells running from the Fitzgerald. They spotted us immediately and the chase was on.

"You gotta move faster than that," I scolded.

"Just try to keep up," Clancy grumbled before diving into the traffic on Main Street.

Horns blared and tires screeched. And Clancy hobbled between traffic like a blind man being led by a cane. The traffic was far less kind to the able-bodied Campbells on our tail. All I heard were horns and curses as Clancy led me into Bull Durham's casino. The slots were empty. The bar was deserted. There was only one table, a poker table, with three lonely patrons. They didn't even flinch as we stumbled through. We were out the back door before a single one of them knew we had passed. The smokers teeming on the back patio were much more curious, especially after we rushed right past them without lighting up. Clancy was hobbling like an Olympic sprinter along the path behind Bull Durham's. It was a curvy path that spit us out right at the intersection of Peak to Peak Highway and Central City Parkway.

We hadn't stepped two feet across the parkway before the sirens began to scream. Red lights flashed off the rocky precipice on the far side of Peak to Peak Highway, warning of approaching law. The sheriff's truck squealed through the intersection as we reached the far sidewalk. Clancy hobbled for the front door of Bullwhackers Casino and I followed him in just as the sheriff's truck screeched to a stop in front of the casino. We made it to the elevator and the doors closed before the sheriff came through the front door.

"Follow me and look normal," Clancy warned as the doors opened.

Clancy calmly walked through the crowd, nodding and greeting everyone that wanted to make eye contact. I followed, in complete panic, eyes darting in every direction, expecting to see the Campbells pouring out of the elevator after us. We made it all the way to the far end of the floor before I saw the elevator doors open. And we were into the stairwell before I saw anyone step out. The only way to go was down. At the bottom of the stairs, we could go left, back onto the casino floor, or right, through an exit door. Clancy went straight for the exit door.

The air was cold and refreshing as we stepped into the alley behind the casino. There was no one to be seen.

"This way," Clancy ushered west towards Central City.

A sense of calm was just about to wash over me when I heard a scuffling of feet rush into the alley from a door about fifty yards back from where we had exited. I didn't even have to turn around to know it was the Campbells.

"They're back here!" a voice cried from behind.

The words had barely echoed down the alley when Clancy darted into the back door of Black Hawk Station. The casino was a museum with two lonely cowboys feeding the slots. The front door spit us right back out on the parkway. The crowd had thinned since we first arrived, and their energy had turned far more hostile. Even the drunks seemed to be yelling out our location. We dove into the front door of the next casino — I didn't catch the name. We were back in the alley in the blink of an eye.

From there my memory is just a blur of casinos and strange faces. Clancy weaved us in and out of casinos from Black Hawk to Central City. At one point we covered three casinos by their roofs. I think we were in Central City. All I remember is following Clancy to the top of a stairwell and cringing when I saw him open the door that warned of alarms that would sound the moment said door was opened. I only remember because of the smirk on Clancy's face when he looked back at me and shoved the door open. He knew I was expecting the alarm to sound. And his eyes shined with pride when it didn't. We were three casinos down, and all the way to the edge of town, with no signs of the Campbells on our tail, when I finally spoke up.

"How the hell'd you do that?"

"Do what?"

"Know exactly where to go."

"I grew up in this town, kid. You think that's the first time I had to ditch the law? Hell, me and my friends planned escape routes from every building in this town." Clancy was almost nostalgic as he looked back over the lights of Central City.

The sky was clear and dark and sprinkled with twinkling stars as the casino lights faded behind us. The road turned from plowed pavement to snow-packed gravel after we passed the casinos' shadows.

"Where we going?" I asked.

"Got some land up the way, should be safe to spend the night."

"How'd they know we were gonna be at Fitzgerald's?"

"Musta tapped the Lost Creek phone booth."

"So, they know you're helping me?"

"S'pose they do."

The wind was strong and against us, blowing frozen ice crystals to sandblast my cheeks. We followed Eureka Street to its end, and continued onto Upper Apex Road. My face went numb after twenty minutes. My cheeks were black with frostbite in thirty. I was certain I would freeze to death long before we reached Clancy's land. But all I could think about was Blue. Sheriff Campbell would certainly send someone to watch Clancy's shack, if he hadn't already. And I had two long and frigid hours to walk uphill into the icy wind to think about poor Blue's certain demise. Two hours in frigid silence is more than enough time to allow the mind to manufacture some really horrible visions. By the time the road really started climbing, I was seeing crystal-clear visions of Blue faithfully protecting Clancy's porch. He growled as unfriendly footsteps approached. From the footsteps, a dark shadow appeared. And just before the face of the shadow was shone in the moonlight, flames flashed and a shot rang out from the shadow's gun. Blue's yelp rang through my head. Then the visions would start over.

"We're almost there," Clancy cried just as we approached a switchback where the road really began to climb. I was relieved for a second, until I saw Clancy climbing over the snow berm to an overgrown trail crusted over with a good four feet of snow. The trail was only a hundred yards, but it must have taken us half an hour to posthole our way to the end. The way Clancy was wheezing, I thought he was going to tip over dead and leave me all alone to fend for myself.

"Almost there?" I questioned when the trail opened on a clearing. "Can you define 'almost'?" The thought of crossing through the deep snow of that frozen clearing had flavored my tone with a fair amount of attitude.

"We're here," Clancy answered as he dropped into the snow.

"We're here? ... Where we gonna sleep?" I once more looked over the clearing, expecting to see some hidden shack that I had previously missed.

"Under good old Colorado," Clancy pointed at the peaks to our west. The jagged peaks were high and far, but they gradually climbed down to a steep precipice that bordered the clearing to the west like a solid rock wall.

"Under Colorado? What the hell are you talking about?"

"That's Colorado Mountain."

"Whatever," I sharply answered. I was in no mood for Clancy's games. He was always making preposterous-sounding claims just to get a rise out of me while slowly feeding me all the facts until it seemed I was an idiot for not believing him. Clancy quickly sensed my agitation and picked himself out of the snow and postholed towards the steep rocky border.

The cliff climbed straight out of the snow at the edge of the clearing. I about threw a fit when Clancy dropped to the snow and started digging.

"A snow cave? ... We walked all this way just to dig a snow cave!?"

Clancy didn't respond and soon his feet were gone. I was growing more furious by the second as I watched Clancy push snow out of his tunnel. "Couldn't we have done this two hours ago... before the frostbite set in?" I was to the point of mumbling curses under my breath when Clancy popped his head out of the tunnel.

"You comin' in or what?" Clancy smirked before descending back into his hole.

I was so angry I almost considered digging my own cave — the thought of curling up with Clancy and listening to him tell his stupid stories till we fell asleep did make me consider it —

but some inner sense quickly pointed out the stupidity in such thoughts.

I followed Clancy into the hole, crawling with rancor. Every move I made, every expression cast, was a demonstration of my protest, exaggerated to catch Clancy's attention — none was paid. Clancy wasn't even there. The cave dead-ended at the sheer rocky cliff. It tunneled left for a few feet, and right for a few more. But there was no Clancy.

"This way!" Clancy suddenly popped his head out of the rocky wall at the end of the left tunnel. He scared the shit out of me. And then his head dropped back into the wall with a wail of cackling at my fear.

I crawled to the end of the left tunnel to find a crack splitting the rocky cliff. It was barely a foot wide at ground level. I had to take off my backpack, push it into the hole, and turn on my side just to squeeze in, pushing the pack ahead of me with my arms as I kicked forward with my legs. Suddenly the crack widened and dropped. My backpack slid down the crevice. The weight, along with the awkward position of my arm, had my fingers straining to hold the pack. I had no leverage to hold it. And in trying to twist my body for better leverage, I rolled right off the ledge and slid head first down the crevice. I thought I was sliding straight to the depths of hell. Not only did it feel like I was falling forever, but I could see the flickering of fire coming from below.

It turns out I only dropped about four feet before falling headfirst onto a pile of sand. Clancy was laughing his ass off as I rolled down the pile.

"Feet first, my boy," Clancy chuckled. "Always go feet first."

When I finally found my feet and gathered my pack, I realized the enormity of Clancy's hideaway. An ancient underground river had carved a ten-feet-wide by thirty-feet-deep cavern, three thousand feet under the peaks of Colorado Mountain — the watermarks on the walls gave evidence of the water levels from some ten thousand years ago. The living room décor presented evidence of far more recent inhabitation. The first thing I thought of was the Flintstones. A big slate of granite, three feet wide by five feet long, set atop pillars of carefully stacked flat rocks, made a dining table. Rock chairs sat on all four sides like thrones, with slate granite backrests and little slate armrests. Above the table, hanging from a hook drilled straight into the rocky ceiling, hung a chandelier of old gas lanterns. The lanterns were just starting to burn hot enough to light the far shadows when Clancy sparked a match.

"Helluva table, huh?"

"Who built it?" I asked, expecting to hear some wild tale about Clancy meeting a family of cavemen whom had never known anything of modern civilization.

"Mostly me," Clancy answered. "My dad helped build a rig to hoist the top up. I was just a scrawny little boy back then. That's the only reason my father brought me out to help him look for a plot of land to buy. It was my job to check the smallest of crevices for caves. My father was convinced that the rivers had been picked clean and caves were the only place that anyone, aside from the big mining companies that carved giant holes into the sides of the mountains with their heavy equipment, could still find gold. We spent the whole summer, hiking all over Gilpin County, looking for the perfect plot. It was a cold morning in September when I found that little crack that led to this cave. Clancy's Cavern, my father called it. He bought the plot that very afternoon. I spent every day that fall fixing this place up."

Clancy's fire was roaring when he finished his story. The fire burned behind a barrier of the same flat rocks that made the legs of the table, tucked under a ledge blackened by previous fires. The flames gave new and growing definition to the far end of the cavern. Clancy was feeding the fire with wood from a pile to the right of the fireplace.

"Now that's some dry wood." Clancy laughed. "Been curing fer fifty years."

"What about the smoke?"

"There's a crack back in there that cuts all the way through the mountain, sucks the smoke right out on the other side."

As the fire brightened, I noticed a black hole in the wall to the left of the fire. It was about two feet off the rocky floor. I stepped closer to investigate. The darkness turned out to be a nook in the wall about six feet long and three feet deep, with a perfectly smooth ledge. Lying on the ledge was a makeshift mattress made of a rainbow of faded canvas bags sewn together and stuffed with tattered old clothing.

"Best not be eyein' me bunk, boy," Clancy warned as I pressed the mattress. "Yer bunk is on the other side."

Directly across the cavern was an almost identical nook, with an almost identical mattress.

"This is where you sleep?" I crawled into Clancy's nook to find myself staring at the rocky ceiling no more than two feet from my nose. I had to slide in sideways. There was no sitting up.

"You learn mighty quick not to jump out of bed in the morning."

"If you don't scramble your brains."

"If I was you, I'd worry 'bout getting them wet clothes dry before morning… Tomorrow's gonna be a long day."

Clancy was already stripped down to his tighty-whities when I crawled from his bunk. His clothes were hanging on a line above the fire. His stinky wet socks sizzled and dripped. He was in his bunk and snoring before I had my jacket hanging on the line.

I cursed Clancy's snoring the entire night. But he really had nothing to do with the fact that I couldn't fall asleep. It was my worry over Blue that kept my mind spinning. I was happy to climb out of my rocky coffin of a bed when the flames flickered into orange coals. The purpose of providing warmth was the only thing keeping my mind off Blue. That's when I got the bright idea to read Darla's diary. My deceitful subconscious swore to me it was the only thing that could take my mind off Blue, but something deep down inside me told me I was actually looking for reasons to justify Darla's actions. She couldn't possibly be held responsible for actions she was raised to believe were normal. I found her fifth or sixth entry to be a perfect example:

Dear Diary,

Daddy's plan worked. I now understand the importance of planning every detail. No one even questioned whether or not Brian's death was an accident. Daddy told me no one would question his death if he crashed during a race. I told him our best chance was during our first practice run, before they put up the netting to block the trees. They always have the netting set up by our second run. All I had to do was get Brian to take a drink from my water bottle before his first lap. Mom laced it with a concentrate of valerenic acid she cooked up from the valerian root in her greenhouse. She said not to give Brian a drink until he was just about to take his first lap. The toxins would render him paralyzed forty-five seconds after he took a drink. From his time trials earlier in the week, we knew he would be in the middle of the course when the V kicked in, right where the trail gets really narrow. Brian lost control right where we expected. The coroner said his head hit the tree at no less than fifty miles per hour. Brian's skull was crushed upon impact. No one even thought to test his blood for toxins. Not that they would have found anything. Daddy says valernic acid isn't even a toxin they test for.

I must have read a dozen of Darla's dairy entries before Clancy crawled from his bunk. Everything I read told me Darla never had a chance. Her parents had taught her how to kill a man at an age when most parents teach their children the golden rule.

"Rise and shine, sleepy head," Clancy chirped with such a chipper tone I honestly thought about choking him — Damn Darla's twisted diary.

"I'm up," I groaned. "Still up."

We dressed and crawled from Clancy's Cavern without saying a word. We had to scale the wall and shimmy up through the same crack I dropped down. It was much tougher to climb up and out than it was to fall down and in. I thought I was going to suffocate by the time we spilled into the stuffy snow cave at the end of the crack. The air was cold and crisp as we waded into Clancy's family meadow.

CHAPTER 9

The sun hadn't even risen above the trees when Clancy proposed murder. He was ready to kill the whole Campbell clan.

"As long as they're alive, we're dead."

"Why don't we just leave the state until this all blows over?"

"And go where?"

"Who cares? As long as we get out of Gilpin County, they can't touch us."

"You sure 'bout that?"

"Yeah," I answered, but my voice was loaded with uncertainty.

"Even if I was sure we'd be safe, which I ain't, there's no way in hell I'm lettin' them bastards run me out of my own town."

"Well, there's no way I'm killing anyone."

"You can't kill the man tryin' to kill you?"

"I can't murder an entire family."

"You don't have to… just half of 'em," Clancy cackled.

My sharp eyes were quick to tell Clancy I was in no mood for jokes.

"It's that Darla, isn't it… you fell fer her, didn't you?"

"No! I didn't fall for her." Even I didn't believe my words.

A strange look of dumbfounded confusion froze Clancy's

face — I thought he was having a stroke. He just stood there, staring at me with glazed eyes.

"Are you crappin' your pants?" I awkwardly joked.

Clancy snapped out of his silence, but he was talking like he was in a trance. "If you knew Darla killed your father, could you kill her?"

"My father?"

"Could you kill her if she killed your father?"

"What are you talking about?"

"Martin was yer father," Clancy claimed with the straightest of faces.

I was not expecting that. I silently glared at Clancy with a rage of emotions swirling like hurricanes behind my eyes. I could tell he could see the turmoil, but he never flinched.

"I'm sorry you had to find out like this," Clancy consoled. "I wasn't supposed to tell you."

"Stop. Just stop." I clinched my fists until my knuckles were throbbing and white. Visions of punching Clancy square across the jaw played through my head a dozen times — if he were thirty years younger I'm certain I would have decked him. Instead, I turned and walked away. I was done with Clancy. I was done with Lost Creek. I didn't care if the Campbells killed another hundred people. I was going to hike out to the road, hitchhike to Lost Creek, find Blue, and get the hell out of this crazy mountain county. But Clancy just kept running his mouth.

"You were born on August 12, right?"

I kept right on walking.

"You were supposed to be born on July 12, am I right?" Clancy hollered at my back. The thought that he was still pushing such preposterous claims stopped me in my tracks. I hadn't even considered his questions when I turned around and charged — I was too busy picturing tackling him. I was in full sprint, just about to lay him out, when I realized I had never told Clancy my birthday. I stopped just before tackling him. Clancy never flinched. The smug smirk on his face told me he knew I would. And I quickly realized where he learned my birthday.

"You're good," I shook my finger in Clancy's face. "How

could Clancy possibly know my birthday?" I mocked. "I know you saw it when you were helping me with my student loans."

"S'pose I could've, but I knew yer birthday long before I ever met ya."

"Really?"

"I ain't shittin' ya, kid. You're a Leo, right?"

"A Leo?"

"Born under the sign of the lion."

"So?"

"So was Martin… All the men born to Martin's family were Leos, going as far back as the records. He always said he was going to write a book about his family history. 'The Pride of Leos,' he was going to call it."

"So, I'm Martin's son because I'm a Leo?" I laughed.

"You're a Leo because you're Martin's son."

I could only shake my head in disbelief at Clancy's claim. I was just about to turn back around and march out of Clancy's life forever when he reminded me of his earlier question for which I had no answer.

"How did I know you were supposed to be born, or rather told that you were supposed to be born, on July 12?"

There was no way Clancy could have known that. I hadn't even thought about it since… I don't even know when.

"I told you that over late-night whiskey in your shack?" I offered.

How the hell did Clancy know that? It was true. My parents had always told me I hung out in the womb for an extra month. I was supposed to be born on the twelfth of July, but I didn't come until the twelfth of August. I was too young to question the absurdity of a ten-month pregnancy. And why would I?

"Yer folks lived in Colorado back in seventy-six, didn't they?"

I was too confused to do anything but nod.

"Yer mother liked to ski?"

She did. I heard many stories as a child about how I was riding the ski slopes of Colorado before I was born.

"What mountain was it that she skied?"

"Winter Park," I answered in a trance.

Clancy continued with a long-drawn tale of how my mother had supposedly met Martin at Winter Park on opening day.

"Snowed two feet the night before. Martin was just strappin' his skis on when yer mother came bombing towards the lift screaming bloody murder and waving her poles like a maniac. She never skied powder before, didn't know how to turn. Everyone else scooted their ass outta the way as she sped straight for the chairlift. Martin was so baked, he didn't even notice. Yer mama smoked him at full speed. Two them tumbled like rag dolls, skis and poles and hats and goggles flyin' everywhere. Martin was just 'bout to give yer mama the hollerin' of her life when he saw her face. It was love at first sight, for Martin," Clancy claimed. "He skied with her for the rest of the day. You were conceived that very afternoon, high on the slopes of Mary Jane." Clancy went on and on. And I was in such a state of shock that I couldn't stop him. He told me all about how Martin and my mother spent every night in November together. He said Pops was away on a job site the entire month. "That's why yer mom always swore you were conceived in October." He even told me he had met my mother — he knew exactly what she looked like. "It was in Martin's shack, the night she told him she was pregnant. She told him she was pregnant with his baby, in one breath, and told him she was moving away to Missouri, in the next. Said she couldn't possibly raise a child in Lost Creek. Said she couldn't have anything to do with Martin. And she made him promise to never interfere in yer life. It was a promise Martin regretted every day that followed. All he asked was that she name you Jack."

I never told Clancy I was born in Missouri. A storm of emotions rushed over me. The mere thought that Clancy could be telling the truth was a concept I couldn't fathom. I stormed off before I could gather a rational thought. I didn't even care that I wasn't following the trail we had blazed the night before. Somehow the strenuous path I had chosen through the deep snow seemed, in my mind, to perfectly express my plight.

"Where you goin'?"

"Gettin' Blue and gettin' the hell out of here."

"You can't go back to the Creek, there's gonna be Campbells all over our shacks."

"Bye, Clancy." I waved a listless wave with my back to Clancy as I stomped through the snowy meadow.

"Yer going the wrong way!"

I wasn't going the wrong way. I was heading east, toward the rising sun, toward Peak to Peak Highway. I wasn't about to walk the whole way to Lost Creek — I was going to hitchhike. I postholed across the meadow and disappeared into the trees, never once turning back to Clancy to give him the satisfaction of knowing he had completely twisted my mind. The snow was just as deep in the trees. It took over an hour before I finally stumbled across a beaten trail. It was heading a bit more north than I wanted, but it sure beat wading through waist deep snow. There was a maze of trails as I ventured forward, old roads from the mining days. I must have spotted a dozen old mine pits. I even came across an old mining camp with the crumbling remains of six log shacks built over a hundred years ago. At one point, about three hours in, when I walked upon a strange forest of fallen trees that rolled like a wave of dead gray, I began to believe Clancy was right — about going the wrong way. Was I so angry I stormed off in the wrong direction? The sun was high in the sky at that point and lent no bearing. My lips were so dry they were cracked and bleeding. My stomach grumbled to remind me just how long it had been since it had been fed.

I was seriously considering curling up against a tree and taking a little nap when I spotted a herd of cattle in a field below. I veered off the trail and into the deep snow to see the Peak to Peak Highway across the field. And a wave of relief washed over me to make me realize just how dire my situation had been. With a newfound energy, I waded through the deep snow to the field with ease. From the edge of the field, I could see a restaurant on the other side of the road. It was the Last Shot Saloon. I had driven by it a few times, but never stopped. And I drooled over the thought of a juicy bacon cheeseburger.

The snow was even deeper across the field, and windblown.

I decided to skirt the field, under the cover of the trees, to conserve the last of my energy. It was a good thing; I was ready to drop dead by the time I climbed the snowplow berm and rolled onto the highway. Everything in me told me to cross the road, hike up until I found a vantage point where I had enough time to spot oncoming cars and decide if they looked safe before sticking out my thumb, but my grumbling stomach won. I crossed the road and walked straight into the Last Shot Saloon. To be honest with you, it wasn't just my stomach that led me in — I had to call my mom. I had to prove Clancy wrong.

The saloon was packed. Every stool at the long log bar was taken. Both pool tables were surrounded. The crowd ranged from old flannelled mountain men to cute young girls. The juke box was rockin'. Everyone was drunk and jolly and having a hell of time — especially for a weekday afternoon. No one even noticed me walk in. I took a lonely table in the back corner and watched the rowdy crowd to make sure no one was watching me. That's when I noticed the shot glasses. Every flat surface was covered with collectable shot glasses from all over the world — thousands of shot glasses. I was pretty sure no one cared that I was there by the time the cute little brunette waitress sauntered over with a menu and water. I sucked the glass dry before she had a chance to speak.

"Looks like some one's thirsty," she smiled.

"You have no idea."

I ordered a bacon cheeseburger with fries, a beer, and another water before the waitress skipped away. I watched her to make sure she wasn't calling the authorities — for all I knew the Campbells had plastered my picture all over the county. She made no suspicious moves and quickly returned with my beer and water.

"Thank you." I immediately grabbed the water. "Is there a payphone around here?"

"Sorry, there isn't."

"Do you think I could make a collect call from the bar phone?"

"They don't let anyone use the phone."

"That's okay," I answered. But the look in my eyes told the sweetheart waitress of my chagrin.

"Who you need to call?"

"My mom," I answered in the most pathetic voice.

That poor waitress melted. "Aww... here, use my phone." The waitress pulled her cell phone from her apron.

"You get service up here?" I perked up.

"If you stand in the far corner on the back deck."

"Thank you, thank you so much... what do I owe you?" I reached for my pocket.

"Don't worry about it, I get unlimited calls — just don't steal it."

I found a signal and dialed my mother's number, chuckling as I thought about how just one year prior, back when I relied on my contacts list, I never would have remembered my mother's phone number. It was an awkward call, to say the least.

"Hey, Ma."

"Jack!?"

"Yeah."

"He's alive." Her voice rang with sarcasm.

"So far."

"How are you? It's been so long."

"It hasn't been that long."

Our conversation continued with awkward small talk about everything from the weather to whether I was eating right. How the hell does one gently turn mother and son small talk into an interrogation of his mother's infidelity? All I know is that turning the conversation straight from "No, Ma, I haven't found a job, yet," to "So... did you have an affair with a man named Martin when you lived in Denver?" is not the way to go. My mother immediately turned offensive. And, just as I suspected, she dispelled Clancy's tales as lies. But the apprehension in her voice was all I needed to question her integrity. I was even more confused when I hung up. I knew Clancy was right. I knew Clancy was a liar. I was certain my mother would never lie to me. I knew she had.

I stepped back to the highway with a satisfied stomach, a

disturbed psyche, a pathetic plan, a one-beer buzz, and my thumb in the air. I was so lost in my thoughts Sheriff Campbell could have come along and picked me up and I wouldn't have noticed. Thankfully, I was only on the side of the road for a couple minutes before the first car stopped. It was a rusted-out Chevy Blazer that wore a rainbow of colors. The passenger door was green. The hood was blue. The tailgate was cherry red. The remaining rusty panels seemed to suggest the original color was black — twenty years ago. A billowing cloud of smoke poured out as I opened the passenger door. The driver was a young stoner from Ned with scraggly blond dreads.

"Where you headed," the young stoner moaned.

"Lost Creek." I slammed the door.

"Lost Creek?" He was baked out of his mind as he pulled onto the highway. "You live in Lost Creek, bro?"

"No, just passin' through." I buckled my seat belt.

"You should pass right on through to Ned, bro."

"Why's that?"

"Bad shit going down in the Creek."

"Oh?" I played dumb. "What kind of shit?"

"I don't know, bro. But when word to stay away from Lost Creek spreads… us Ned Heads stay away from Lost Creek."

"Really? Maybe you could drop me off at the bridge before town?"

"Sure thing, bro."

I had my new stoner friend drop me off at the last curve before Lost Creek in case the Campbells were watching the road. Then I ran for the ridge to make sure he didn't get stopped going through town. He wasn't stopped, and the town looked quiet. I followed the trees to the river and followed the river all the way to Clancy's property.

The river's trickle lulled me into a false sense of serenity. If not for a fluttering ptarmigan that nearly gave me a heart attack and sent me diving into a drift, I probably would have walked right to Clancy's front door. I was at the edge of the clearing in front of Clancy's when my surroundings and my predicament returned to focus. But instead of surveying the grounds for riflemen, my eyes ominously scanned the pristine white for the bloody red puddles of Blue's last stand. My eyes searched every inch surrounding Clancy's shack. I saw no red. And no signs of Blue.

After what felt like at least twenty anxious minutes, I decided it was safe to approach. Looking back, I don't think my mind had looked for anything other than red. I made it to within ten yards from Clancy's shack before a noise stole my attention from the snowy white ground. It sounded like it came from in front of me, but there was nothing between me and the shack. I was just about to turn around and survey the grounds behind me when my mind detected an anomaly — the window was slightly cracked. Clancy never opened the window after October. The thought had barely processed when my eyes focused on the shiny black barrel resting on the window sill. It was pointing straight at me. And before I could process the horror, a firestorm roared from the barrel in slow motion. It felt like I had forever to dive for cover. But I couldn't move. And the warm rush of a rifle's report washed over my face.

I was still standing in place, with the dumbest of looks on my face, when Clancy stomped onto his porch.

"Get in here, Dumbass!"

I thought I was dead. It hadn't even dawned on me that Clancy had killed a Campbell less the ten yards behind me. I was still feeling my stomach, expecting to find that my bowels had been blown out over the snow behind me, when I turned to see Mike Campbell bubbling with red death from his chest, choking and dying in the snow.

I was still standing, jaw dropped, when Clancy rushed over, grabbed my arm, and yanked me into his shack.

"Two minutes!?" Clancy scolded. "I thought I taught you to survey the perimeter for at least thirty before making your approach."

"I did," I answered automatically.

"The hell you did."

I had no further argument. I knew I had no awareness of what I was walking into. Clancy scolded me for what must have been a good five minutes. All I could do was take it. He went on to tell me all about how big of an idiot I was for hiking towards the highway instead of heading straight north for Lost Creek. Apparently, he had made it to his shack hours before I arrived. He said I had hiked three times further just to reach Peak to Peak Highway.

"You woulda waited five more minutes, you would have found Blue wading through my meadow.

"You found Blue!?" I finally perked up.

"You gotta be shittin' me?!"

"What?"

"Out of everything thing I just said, the only thing you heard was that I saw Blue?"

"Where?"

"Jesus, Jack, you're worse than Martin."

"Is he okay?"

"He was damn near dead when I found him. That dumbass dog musta been trackin' yer scent all night."

"Where is he?"

Clancy's face turned grim.

"What?"

Clancy remained silent and stepped to the kitchen table. Then he shoved the table aside, turned to me with a sinister smile, and opened the trap door in the floor. Blue sprung out in one leap and tackled me.

"Did you come looking for me?" I asked like I was talking to a toddler. "Such a good boy, Blue."

Blue stepped back and started pawing at his face. Clancy had somehow tied a leather strap around his snout.

"What the hell?" I yelled as I pulled it off.

"Damn dog started making a hell of a commotion about thirty minutes ago… Musta smelled you coming."

Blue practically licked the skin off my face when I removed the strap. Then he stepped back to scold me with his sharp bark.

"Shut that damn dog up," Clancy whispered as he raced to the window. The glass shattered with a barrage of gunfire just as he looked out. Clancy dropped to the floor so fast I thought he was shot.

"Are you hit?"

"Get down, dumbass!"

I dove to the floor. Clancy hadn't been hit, except by a piece of flying glass that cut his cheek.

The Campbells had the shack surrounded. We were pinned to the floor under a constant barrage of gunfire. They had some serious automatic firepower. They must have pumped a thousand rounds into the shack. The only break in the thundering assault was the few seconds between clips. The door was peppered with holes spilling bright beams of mountain sunlight into the shack like little white lasers beaming through the dusty air when the shooting finally stopped.

"This is it, boy." Clancy crawled across the shattered debris to pass me a rifle.

"What do I do?"

"Shoot anything that moves."

Clancy watched the south and west side from the kitchen window. I watched the east and south from small cracks between the logs on the southeast corner. We were completely blind to the north — not that I could really see anything through little cracks in the wall. I could, however, hear them talking. I couldn't understand the words, but I could tell they were making a plan. Then the voices went silent. I heard footsteps crunching through the snow, but I couldn't see anyone approaching. BANG! Clancy's rifle echoed through the shack. The thud of a body dropping on the steps was muted by shattering glass, and then a WHOMPF of fire. My south side crack was glowing with flames. And the wretched screaming that followed told me a man was burning to death on Clancy's porch from a Molotov cocktail he wasn't able to toss before Clancy shot him in the gut. A single shot rang from the tree line to kill the screaming. A barrage of gunfire followed to keep us pinned to the floor. That's when a shattering burst of flames roared in Clancy's shack. The fumes and the flames and the smoke quickly engulfed the entire shack.

"Time to go," Clancy shouted as he jumped into the trap

door in the floor. "Grab the gun bag."

I grabbed the gun bag and dove for the trapdoor as the flames rolled across the floor on a wave of gasoline.

"Blue, come!" I screamed as I looked back to see Blue crouching in the corner. "Come on, boy. It's okay."

"Leave the damn dog," Clancy grumbled.

"I can't."

"We gotta go." Clancy was pulling me down the hole.

I let out my best inside out whistle and Blue's fears were overcome by his instincts. He sprung from the corner and leapt over the flames to land right on top of me.

The floorboards were already glowing orange above us as Clancy removed a piece of plywood to reveal a tunnel that was maybe two feet high and three feet wide. We had to crawl on our bellies until the tunnel finally widened. Even then, it was only about four feet high.

"Never thought I'd actually have to use that," Clancy chuckled as he lit a lantern.

"You dug that?"

"Been cuttin' that tunnel for twenty some years."

"Why?" I started to ask, until I noticed the walls sparkling golden from the lantern's light.

"Found a hell of a vein," Clancy chuckled.

The tunnel tapered down to nothing more than a crack in the wall, barely wide enough to squeeze through. On the other side of the crack was Clancy's cooler. The thought of hiding out in the same place we had butchered another animal just a few months prior was seriously creepy. But stepping outside with dozens of Campbells ready to shoot us dead sounded like a much worse idea. Clancy felt differently.

"My old shack will be noting but ashes soon. It won't take long for the sheriff to realize our charred bodies aren't amongst the remains."

"We could hold them off. There's only room for one of them to come through on either side. We could each watch an entrance, pick 'em off one at a time."

"Until they smoke us out."

I hadn't thought of that. And then I realized I had really screwed up.

"I forgot the gun bag."

"What!?"

"I forgot the gun bag in the trap door chamber."

"We gotta go back." Clancy was just starting to climb up the crack when a barrage of gunfire rang from above. "Dammit!" Clancy cried as he dropped back down.

"What's wrong?"

"You deaf now, too? That's our ammunition burning up in the fire."

"I'm sorry, Clancy."

"Yer gonna be," Clancy grumbled as he headed for the exit.

We waited silently in the shadow of the entrance to Clancy's cooler until the sun's last light was lost to the mountain's darkness. And then we army-crawled through the deep snow until we hit the tree line where we ran straight for the river. I thought Clancy was going to have a heart attack. I was panting and sweating. Even Blue was winded. But we didn't dare stop to catch our breath until we reached the river.

"Walk the rocks," Clancy whispered as he hopped onto an icy rock on the edge of the river.

We hopped from rock to icy rock for about fifty yards and then climbed the ridge where I first saw Clancy.

"Now we wait," Clancy whispered when we reached the top.

Nothing but a pale crescent moon lit the night as we perched high above the river to make sure no one was following our tracks. The barrage of exploding ammunition from Clancy's stockpile kept the Campbells from investigating the charred rubble until long after dark.

"I can't see shit," I whined."

"Shhh! You gotta listen."

We listened to the wind whistle and the last rounds of Clancy's armory explode for thirty minutes as the sweat rolling down my back turned to ice.

"I don't think they're following us," my teeth finally chattered.

"Shhh!"

We sat there for another fifteen freezing minutes before he led us on.

We hopped rocks upriver for another hour. My boots were soaked and frozen over. Poor Blue was one big icicle. But Clancy kept marching on. We were past the tunnel when my legs went completely numb.

"We need to start a fire," I cried.

"Just a little further."

"A little further" was another hour. He finally stopped at a little tin shack nestled into the trees about a hundred yards from the river. The tiny shack made Clancy's look like a hotel. Most Minnesota icehouses are bigger.

"It's locked," I said as I flipped the rusty padlock.

"I have a key," Clancy casually replied before grabbing a rock and smashing the lock.

The inside of the shack was about ten feet by ten feet, with a broken bunk against one wall and a rusty old barrel stove against the other. The tin chimney pipe had long ago fallen from the ceiling and was lying on the floor.

"We need dry kindling," Clancy ordered as he gathered the pipe. "I'll get this stove working."

The little tin shack was toasty within minutes of lighting the fire. It reeked of wet dog and sweaty balls, soon after. And, even with all the chaos surrounding us, all I could think about was how silly Clancy and I must look. Old man Clancy was stripped down to his tattered tighty-whities. I was down to my soggy boxers. And our wet clothing was hanging all about the shack.

"You should get some sleep… gonna be a long day tomorrow," Clancy warned as he counted his few rounds.

"Where we gonna go?"

"We're not going anywhere."

"We just gonna stay here forever?"

"Just till it's over."

"How long's that gonna be?"

"Till we kill 'em all."

"With what?" We only had one rifle, with only six rounds,

and a pistol with one clip.

"We're gonna have to get creative."

"There's no way we're getting anywhere near the Campbells without getting killed."

"No need. They'll be here in a few hours."

"What? … Why?"

"Sheriff Campbell's no idiot; he'll be on our tracks at first light."

"What tracks? We walked up the river the whole way."

"That'll only slow down a tracker like Campbell by an hour at best."

Every crackle of our dying fire, every howl of wind, every creak and every crack, I was certain the Campbells were surrounding the shack. It was the longest night of my life. And because I'm an idiot, I read Darla's diary to distract my mind:

Dear Diary,

Best Birthday Ever. I got a cake. I had a party. Dad bought me a new Jeep. But my best present was from myself. I got to kill Jeremy Hanson. What a worthless piece of shit. Mom will be so proud. I used her hemlock seeds just like she taught me. And Dad didn't even have to cover for me this time. He didn't even know. Everyone thinks Jeremy drowned. I knew they would. I thought about everything this time. I made sure Jeremy told no one we were meeting. I told him I stole a quarter pound of Uncle Charlie's weed and would sell it to him cheap. I knew he'd want to try it. I ground up nine seeds into a fine powder, mixed it with the pot, and rolled a joint. Mom's hemlock seed frosting recipe called for only six seeds, but that was to be eaten. Unsure if smoking it would be as effective, I used nine. Six would have been plenty. I think even three would've sufficed. Jeremy was grasping his throat after the first hit. He barely coughed out, 'This shit tastes funny,' before his face turned red and his eyes bulged bright white and intense. Then he started to shake and his eyes dulled to a glossy gray. His face was blue when he dropped to the ground. I had him meet me at Clear Creek rapids because I knew there would be no one there this time of year — and I knew the river was deep enough that drowning was plausible. But I never thought Jeremy would make it so easy for me. He hit the ground, shaking and seizing, and crappie flopped right into the river. I thought for sure I was going to have to roll his fat ass into the water. He was even kind enough to have his fishing gear in his truck. I casted his line into a tree on the other side of the river, tangled his pole into the brush hanging over the water, and set his tackle box on the bank. I was barely home in time for dinner when Daddy got the call. A gold panner spotted his body hung up on the rocks in Mayhem Gulch. I can't wait to go to school tomorrow and hear all about it.

For some reason the picture in my head of the gold panner that found the body was of Clancy. Picturing Clancy made me think about Martin. And thinking about Martin made me wonder if his murder had made Darla's diary. I skimmed every page in search of his name. It wasn't there. But I did recognize the name Randy Talbert in her last entry:

Dear Diary,

Randy Talbert will no longer bother Father. But I would be lying if I didn't admit I was a little disappointed about how he went. The asshole killed himself before my poison got a chance. Father said it was perfect. I suppose he's right. No one even thought to think about foul play after Randy ran through town shooting at imaginary monsters before turning his gun to his mouth. I just wish I would've gotten to see the look on his face. I bet the fear in his eyes was priceless. I wish I could've heard the thoughts swirling through his head as he pulled the trigger. I bet he never expected the candy I tossed him during the Dead Guy parade would take him for such a trip. And I never expected it to hit him so fast. The confidence in his gaze turned to straight fear less than five minutes after he ate it. He was a raving lunatic in less than ten. I did get a kick out of watching him swing at invisible demons. The way he was screaming just before he put the barrel in his mouth gave me goose bumps. But I missed that glazed look of defeat that always clouds a man's eyes when he realizes he's been killed by a tiny little lady.

CHAPTER 10

I awoke in a panic to the sound of Clancy cocking his rifle.
The fire had died and the shack was pitch black.

"Rise and shine, sleepyhead."

"What time is it?"

"Time to get yer ass up." Clancy kicked the tin door open
and blindly pointed his rifle into the hazy dawn. "They'll be here
soon."

The approaching dawn provided just enough light to
illuminate Clancy's pale naked body pointing a rifle into the
darkness. His tighty-whities looked yellow compared to his skin.

"Maybe you should put some pants on then." I grumbled.

"Maybe you should stop being a smartass and stoke the fire."

"I thought we were leaving?"

I thought Clancy was going to kill me with his eyes. I got
dressed and stoked the fire without saying another word. Clancy
got dressed, spun the bunk sideways, leaned it against the door,
and then ushered me out before slamming the door behind us.
The bunk slid down and blocked the door so we couldn't get
back in.

"Just in case the Sheriff tries to kick down the door with guns
a blazin'." Clancy pointed to the smoke pouring from the
chimney. "The smoke will make them think we're still in there."

I was crabby, tired, and hungry when we snuck away from our little tin hideaway. We had to walk backwards, in our exact footsteps, all the way to the river. Clancy said there couldn't be any tracks leading away from the shack. He even made me carry Blue's fat ass the whole way. And Blue was angrier than me at Clancy's insistence. He squirmed and grumbled and made it as difficult as he possibly could. My arms were tingling by the time we finally reached the river.

"Don't get your feet wet," Clancy said, as he hopped onto a rock.

We were heading further upriver. I was only two rocks up the river, hopping for a third, when I slipped and my left foot splashed into the icy water. It was only about six inches deep, but that was just high enough for the frigid water to spill over the top of my boot and fill it full. We weren't more than a couple hundred yards up the creek when gunfire rang through the canyon. The sheriff had found the tiny tin shack — the echoed pinging of the bullets hitting the tin was a dead giveaway.

"Forget the river!" Clancy jumped to shore and bounded through the deep snow like a mule deer. I followed, much less gracefully, as my left boot froze to a heavy block. Snow instantly stuck to my frozen boot until it doubled in size. When the gunfire finally died, Clancy stopped running.

"They'll be on our ass any minute," Clancy wheezed.

"What do we do?" I gasped. I think I was even more winded than Clancy.

"We're gonna have so set up an ambush right here."

"There must be a dozen of them!"

"Nine. I picked off three of them bastards before they burned down my shack."

"Nine, whatever. How the hell are we going to kill nine men with six rounds?"

"We got eighteen."

"You think I'm gonna get close enough to shoot someone with this little thing," I whined as I held up the .9mm Clancy gave me.

"Nope," Clancy answered as he grabbed the handgun from

me. "You're on rifle duty."

"Why me?" I asked as he handed me the rifle.

"Ain't no way I can climb to the top of that ridge before they get here," Clancy pointed to the ridge to the west.

Clancy's big plan was for me to climb to the top of the ridge and pick them off as they approached. He was going to circle back around and dig in behind them to take out anyone trying to retreat. "Take yer shots carefully. You can't miss. I can't handle more than three them bastards."

As disturbing as the thought of sighting a human being down the end of that rifle, the thought of waiting down below, in the middle of a swarm of Campbells, with nothing more than a knife and a handgun sounded much more treacherous. I threw the rifle over my shoulder and marched for the ridge without rebuttal. It was a steep climb and the snow was drifted four feet deep. I wasn't perched up on the ridge for more than a minute before Blue started growling. I was still sweating and gasping from the climb. I still hadn't caught my breath when I saw the Campbell posse find our tracks running from the river. There were only eight of them left as their heads came into shaky focus in my scope. They had spread out into a big V like a flock of geese. The leader would take a few steps, stop, look around, signal the flock to follow, and then take a few more steps. The furthest Campbell, the one on the left side of the wing, walked less than ten yards from where Clancy had dug himself down behind a pile of rocks. I was certain he was going to spot Clancy before the group passed the tree that Clancy warned was the range of my rifle. He never saw Clancy.

The leader of the V was a large man wearing a full camouflage suit. He wasn't wearing the uniform, but I was sure it was the sheriff. And it was all I could do to make myself wait until the tail of the flock passed the tree without gunning him down. Every last bit of sense told me to start at the back of the pack, thinking no one could retreat out of range, but emotion beat out sense and I decided the sheriff would get the first bullet. I planned my shots just like Clancy had instructed. I trained my sights on the leader, then I panned over to the man bringing up the right rear — there was one more man on that side. The left rear was next in my sights. I figured I would work my way up that wing since they were closest to Clancy.

With my shots planned out, I settled my sights on the leader of the pack. I had the crosshairs aimed right between his eyes. I wanted to blow that bastard's head clean off. But Clancy's instructions were quick to return perspective. "Aim for the chest," his voice grumbled through my head. So, I dropped the bead to cross squarely over his heart. "Take a deep breath. Hold it in... Slowly squeeze the trigger."

I honestly don't remember squeezing the trigger that first time. I do remember watching the leader drop. My memories are as flickery as an old movie after that. I don't remember taking aim on my second target, but I remember the echo of my shot. I remember seeing him drop. He was in full sprint and slid to a bloody white stop just before the tree he was running to for cover. My third shot blasted a half a second later. It was like I was on autopilot. I don't think I was even looking through the scope. I just swung the barrel hard left and fired. The third Campbell dropped. I missed my fourth shot and hit a tree. Things slowed down after that. The silence was almost spooky. I waved my rifle back and forth, looking through the scope, but I could not spot the remaining five. Then I saw gunfire from Clancy's hiding spot; the sound seemed to echo a long second after the fiery blast. Fire and gunshots rang out in response. Four gunmen were firing into the rocks guarding Clancy. I immediately took aim on the gunman closest to Clancy. I pulled the trigger and he dropped. The last three were well hidden behind trees. I was just about to get up and run down the ridge to help Clancy when one of the three started army-crawling towards Clancy. It was an easy shot. Suddenly, Blue was growling behind me. I looked back to see his coat was in full mohawk. That's when I heard the metallic click of a hammer being cocked. Sheriff Campbell, in full uniform, was staring down at me past the long shiny barrel of a .45 — the barrel must have been ten inches long. I sprung to my feet and raised my rifle, even though I knew it was empty.

"Don't be stupid, boy," Sheriff Campbell warned. "You're empty." The sheriff eyed my bolt. "You put up a hell of a fight, for a flatlander, but these are our mountains."

A barrage of gunfire roared from below. The reports did not sound like they were coming from Clancy's handgun.

"Sounds like old man Clancy's finally told his last tale," Sheriff Campbell gloated as he stepped toward me.

Blue let out a fierce growl.

"Think you're tougher than a bullet, dog?" Sheriff Campbell dropped his sights to Blue.

"No!" I dropped my rifle and jumped in front of Blue. "Leave him alone. I'll do anything you want, just promise me you'll let him go."

"All I want you to do is die. I ain't gotta promise shit to make that happen," the sheriff laughed as he returned his sights to my head. "Front or back?"

"What?"

"You wanna see it coming or not? Normally I wouldn't ask, but my daughter really seemed to like you."

Picturing your own brains being blown out, from both front and back, and trying to choose which would be less painful, has got to be one of the most horrible ways to spend your last moments.

"Time's up."

"What if I just left town, right now, I won't tell anyone. I promise."

Sheriff Campbell roared with laughter at such absurdity.

"Really, I won't say a word," I cried. "I think the way you've kept the riffraff out of your town is a good thing."

"Turn around!"

"Please don't."

"Tell you what, you walk over there to the edge so I don't have to roll you all the way over there to toss you off and I promise I won't shoot your dog."

"You promise?"

"I promise."

Blue grumbled his disapproval.

"Okay."

I knelt down to rub Blue's ears one last time. "You're the best dog in the whole world, Blue. You be a good boy, okay?"

"I ain't got all day."

"Okay. Okay." I waved off the sheriff. "Go find Clancy, Blue." I stood up. "Go on, go find Clancy."

Blue didn't budge. I knew he would attack the moment the sheriff shot me. And I knew the sheriff would shoot him if he did, even if he actually meant to keep his promise.

"Go on, Blue," I shooed. "Go get Clancy."

"You don't really think that dumb dog knows what you're saying?"

"There's Martin!" I pointed to the valley below. Blue's ears perked. "Martin's down there. Go get Martin!"

Blue spun in circles and ran off, bounding through the deep snow down the ridge.

A strange sense of acceptance washed over me as I stepped to the cliff's edge. Despite the fact that I was staring down the barrel of a gun, with visions of my brains being blown out of my skull, it truly was a beautiful day. The sun was high and hot and glowing to warm my frostbitten face. The soothing blue sky seemed to mute the bellows of death from below, and the peaceful sounds of the forest suddenly came alive. I could hear the creek trickling in the distance. Squirrels squawked and chirped and chased in the trees behind me. A pair of gray jays chattered and whistled back and forth from the thick green canopy below. And then came the rumbling. It wasn't a sound I could immediately discern. A rumbling growl is the best way I can describe it. And then it hit me. I knew where I heard that sound before — the night Blue chased the coyote off the porch. I spun around to see Blue sailing through the air in a burst of snow dust. Sheriff Campbell spun around at the same time. BANG! Fire roared from the sheriff's barrel. Blue's fangs sunk into his arm. The shiny silver .45 went sailing through the air. I dove for the gun, but it slid over the edge before I could grab it. I turned back to see Blue still latched onto the sheriff's arm, shaking and shredding. The sheriff was covered in blood. Then

Blue tipped over with blood pouring from a hole in his belly. The Sheriff shoved Blue off his chest, got to his knees and wrapped his arms around Blue's head. He was just about to snap Blue's neck when I tackled him. Things get a bit fuzzy after that. I know we wrestled around in the snow. I know we exchanged quite a few punches. I remember the sheriff getting me in some sort of choke hold; the lights were just about out. But I don't remember pulling my knife from my belt. And I'll never forget the warm wash of blood that flowed over my hand as I sunk the blade deep into the sheriff's belly. His eyes looked so surprised as he dropped face first in the snow.

Poor Blue was whimpering and crying as the bright red blood puddled in the snow around him. I ripped off my jacket and tied it tightly around his waist to stop the bleeding. His body was limp and lifeless when I threw him over my shoulders. I ran down the ridge as fast as I could, with Blue grumbling and moaning from the jostling and his warm blood soaking through my sweater and running down my back. I was huffing and puffing by the time I reached the bottom of the ridge, but I couldn't stop running. I did slow down just enough to grab the rifle from the dead hands of the leader of the V when I passed — that's when I realized it was Sheriff Campbell's son, Bill. I kept right on running through the bloody battlefield. I was back to a full sprint when Clancy jumped from behind a tree.

"STOP!"

I stopped just in time to find myself staring straight down into a ten-foot-deep hole where Darla's cousin, Jerry, was bleeding and moaning with sharpened sticks poking out his back.

"Spotted the old pit while you was takin' yer sweet ass time climbin' the ridge," Clancy laughed. "Barely got them sticks whittled before I heard 'em at the river... Didn't think I had enough."

"Looks like you had plenty." I counted six bloody sticks jammed through Jerry's back before looking away when he started gurgling and drowning in a pool of his own blood.

"Damn near didn't get it covered before that one guy was almost right on top of me. Thought the dumb bastard was gonna go and step in it right off the bat. That would've gotten messy. Look at that," Clancy pointed at a set of tracks about ten feet from the pit, "that's where he passed. Thought fer sure he was gonna spot my tracks."

"Sorry I missed him," I whimpered as I looked at the shattered bark of the tree I shot.

"Hell no, kid, you did great. Fine shootin'. That the sheriff up in front you took first?"

"That's what I thought. Turns out it was his son, Bill. The sheriff circled around and snuck up on me from behind. I'd be dead if it wasn't for Blue."

"He dead?"

"He's gonna be if I don't get him to a vet, soon."

"Not the dog, the sheriff."

"Yeah. I stabbed him."

"Where?"

"Up there on the ridge."

"Where on his body!"

"Sorry. His stomach."

"In the gut!? You make sure he was dead?"

"I didn't check his pulse, if that's what you mean."

"Dammit, boy!" Clancy grabbed the rifle from one of the dead Campbells' hands. "A man can live fer days with a gut wound." Clancy slid back the bolt to check for bullets in the chamber.

"He was face down, dead in the snow. If you want to go check on him, be my guest. I've gotta get Blue to a vet." I turned and started running for my shack just as Clancy turned and stomped towards the ridge.

"Drop it!"

I stopped and turned back around to see the sheriff stepping out from behind a tree with a black revolver pointed at Clancy's head.

"Sheriff ain't lookin' so dead, Jack." Clancy dropped the rifle.

The sheriff quickly wrapped him up in a headlock and pressed his revolver tight to Clancy's ear. I raised my rifle and took aim at the sheriff's head.

"Drop the gun, son," Sheriff Campbell calmly requested.

"Shoot 'm, boy, right between the eyes." Clancy yelled.

"Don't be stupid, son. Even if you do hit me and not him, my reflexes will pull the trigger and the old man dies. Seen it a hundred times." Sheriff Campbell cocked the hammer.

What the Sheriff said seemed to make sense. Worse than that, I knew there was no way I could hit him. Even if I wasn't off-balance because Blue was slumped over my shoulders, my nerves had me so shaky there was no way I could take the shot. The crosshairs bounced from Clancy's right ear to the sheriff's left.

"Shoot him!"

"You do and your friend is dead."

I dropped my sights down to the Sheriff's chest. I think I thought I would be less likely to kill Clancy that way. And when I saw the Sheriff's golden badge shimmer in the sunlight, I took it as a sign. It was the perfect target. I laid the crosshairs right over the center of the star. I didn't take a deep breath. I didn't hold it in. I think I might have closed my eyes. I jerked the trigger. And I shot Clancy right in the arm. The way he dropped, I thought I had killed him.

"Dammit, boy, I said shoot him in the head," Clancy moaned from the ground.

"Sorry," I whimpered.

"Didn't think you had the balls, son," Sheriff Campbell snickered.

"Thought your reflexes would make you pull the trigger?" I fired back. "Seen it a hundred times… You must be gettin' old, Sheriff."

"I may be gettin' old, but I know to check my weapon for rounds before a battle."

"Nice try, Sheriff." I stared down the barrel of the rifle, into his cold grey eyes. I knew exactly what he was trying to do.

"That Bill's rifle?"

"Sure is."

"Only holds seven rounds. You sure you got any bullets left?"

"I dropped your son with my first shot. He dropped like a sack of shit. Never fired a single shot. He never even knew what hit him," I returned with a strange confidence. I have no idea where that came from. I didn't even sound like myself. I was suddenly an outlaw cowboy facing the corrupt sheriff.

"Too bad you're halfcocked."

"So?"

"You even know what that means?" Campbell laughed.

"Yeah?" I had no idea.

"You pull the trigger, ain't nothin' gonna happen."

I could see by the grin building on the sheriff's face that my confidence had obviously faded to doubt.

"He's full of shit, kid," Clancy groaned. "That thing's a semi-automatic."

Sheriff Campbell's face returned the favor. He was full of shit. And then I saw a strange glimmer in his eyes. It somehow beamed his intentions straight to my brain. I squeezed the trigger before I even realized.

Two shots rang out. Sheriff Campbell lowered his gun. I dropped my rifle. I was sure he had hit me. I didn't feel anything, but that's what I thought happened when you died. I didn't see a single hole in the sheriff, aside from the blood-soaked tourniquet around his waist. And the smile on his face said he saw a hole in me. I was just about to drop to my knees when I saw the blood-red circle growing around his badge. The sheriff dropped his gun. Then he fell dead in the snow — I checked his pulse to make sure.

"A little help," Clancy grumbled as he tried to pick himself up.

"I'm so sorry, Clancy," I apologized, over and over, as I helped him up.

"Just a through and through, I'll be fine."

"You sure?"

"Yeah, yeah. Just go." He could tell I was more concerned about Blue.

I sprinted back to my shack. Blue was no longer grumbling and moaning about the jostling. He was unconscious when I laid him on the passenger seat of my truck.

"Don't you die on me, Blue!" I screamed over and over as I raced down the hill towards Nederland.

"He's been shot!" I screamed as I kicked open the front door of the vet's office. It looked more like a barn stall than a medical facility. There was no one around. "Hello!"

"What the heck's goin' on out there?" a gravelly voice hollered from the back room.

"Someone shot my dog," I cried as a tall man with long wavy white hair ducked under the doorframe from the back room.

"Bring him in here." He led me to the operating stall.

Blue was hardly breathing when I set him on the cold steel table. He couldn't keep his eyes open.

"You're a good boy, Blue. You're gonna be fine."

His eyes flickered open one last time to see that I was lying. It was clear across my face. The vet stuck him with a syringe and Blue's eyes faded.

"I love you, Blue."

"Shelly!" the vet screamed.

"Coming," she replied from the back.

"You're gonna want to wait outside for this." The vet turned to me with a mask on his face and a scalpel in his hand. "I'm going to have to cut him open to see how extensive the internal damage is before I'll know if there's anything I can do."

"What is it, Doctor Bob?" Shelly scurried in as I backed out.

I paced back and forth on the creaky barnwood floor of the waiting room for the longest thirty minutes of my life before Shelly came out wearing a blood-smeared apron. The grim look on her face told me she had bad news. I was certain she was going to tell me Blue was dead. Instead of sorrow, a strange anger boiled my blood. Someone had to pay. I immediately thought of Darla.

"He's a tough dog," Shelly's voice interrupted my anger. "He's still fighting."

"Is he going to make it?"

"He's lost a lot of blood. The bullet tore quite a chunk out of his intestines. It's going to take at least an hour, probably two to get everything stitched back together. But Doctor Bob says if Blue can hold on that long, there's a chance he'll make it."

I stormed out of the vet's office with one thought on my mind — Kill Darla Campbell. I raced up the hill into Lost Creek with nothing more than that thought playing through my mind. I pictured it all the way up the hill. I was going to shoot her the moment she opened the door. "That's for Martin!" I screamed after shooting her in the stomach. "And this is for Blue!" I put a bullet in her head. It was easy in my imagination. In reality, I couldn't even pull my gun. I had Clancy's .9mm in my jacket pocket, with my finger on the trigger, as I stepped to her door. I parked my truck at the end of the driveway so she wouldn't know it was me. Then she opened her door and smiled when she saw it was me. She ruined everything.

"Jack! I wasn't expecting you. How are you?" Her voice was cheery and chipper and implied she had no idea of the horrors that had happened.

"I'm alive."

"You sure are… Come in."

I followed Darla all the way to her kitchen before realizing I was in way over my head.

"How do you do it?" I asked.

"Do what?"

"Kill with no remorse."

"I've never killed anyone."

"I read your diary."

Darla turned stone silent.

"Have you seen my dad?" she finally muttered. "Mom and I haven't heard from him."

"Daddy's not gonna be able to save you, this time."

"Is he dead?"

"I'm pretty sure."

"Did you kill him?"

"I did."

"Thank you." Her words were so sincere. I nodded my head like I had done it just for her. And for a slight moment, I almost believed that Darla was the victim. "I'm so sorry I got you involved in this. I never meant to hurt anyone who didn't deserve it."

I almost believed her. The sorrowful look in her eyes was very convincing. But reality quickly washed away such stupidity.

"My father didn't deserve it!"

"Your father?"

"Martin!"

"Martin was your father? You never told me."

"I never knew."

The news that Martin was my father seemed to be almost as much of a shock to her as it was to me. To be honest with you, I still didn't have any proof, but deep down I knew it was true the moment Clancy said it.

"I'm sorry, Jack. I liked Martin, everybody did."

"Then why'd you kill him!"

"Daddy made me do it. He would have killed me if I didn't." Darla reached for my arm.

"Don't."

"But I love you."

"You love me? You'd kill me first chance you got."

"I could never hurt you. I love you. You can't tell me you don't feel it."

"All I feel is betrayed."

Darla covered her teary eyes with her hands and turned away. "Just do it already," she whimpered.

"Do what?" I asked like I didn't know what she was talking about.

"Kill me." Darla turned back to face me. "That's why you came here, isn't it?"

I didn't know what to say.

"What are you waiting for?" Darla's sad tone turned angry.

"How many people have you killed?"

"What does it matter?"

"How many?"

"Forty-six, alright! I've killed forty-six people. And I don't regret a single one. Is that what you wanted to hear? Is that what you needed to be able to do it? Now why don't you take that gun out of your pocket, point it at my head, and pull the trigger?"

BEEP! The oven timer screamed. I was so alarmed I almost accidentally pulled the trigger.

"Pie's done." Darla's demeanor was suddenly cheery. She trotted over to the oven and pulled out a pie. It smelled so good. "Would you like a slice?" Darla pulled a large knife from the knife block, "of pie?"

"Not a chance."

"You sure? It's peach, your favorite. I just whipped up a fresh batch of my homemade whipping cream."

"One of your mother's recipes?"

"It's my recipe. You've had it."

"I'll pass."

"You mind if I have a slice?" Darla held the knife over the pie.

"Go ahead."

"Normally I would let it set for about twenty minutes to thicken up a bit, but I'm guessing I don't have that long?" Darla cut herself a big slice of pie, globed a heavy dollop of whipping cream on top, and shoveled a forkful into her mouth, covering her lips with whipping cream. "Mmm, so good and warm," she said, licking the cream from her lips. "You sure you don't want a piece?"

I didn't know whether I wanted to kill her, eat her pie, or rip off her clothes. I pictured all scenarios, over and over, and with each teasing bite, ripping off her clothes was overcoming.

"I know what you're doing," I finally charged.

"What? I'm just trying to enjoy my last meal." Darla licked her lips.

"Who, me?" I mocked, licking my lips. "I'm just too cute to be anything other than innocent."

"You look like you could use a drink; you want a beer?" Darla reached for the fridge.

"No! I don't want a beer."

"Come on, have one last beer with me." Darla grabbed two bottles from the fridge and set them on the counter. "They're all sealed up, if that's what you're worried about." She tapped the metal caps with the tip of her knife before prying open both bottles with the blade. "It's there if you want it," she said, sliding one of the bottles towards me.

A cold beer had never sounded so good. Hell, I was so thirsty, I even thought about licking the sweat off the outside of the bottle. But in my mind, Darla had already considered that and laced the outside of the bottle with some sort of poison. As I watched Darla chug her beer, I realized there was no way I was going to be able to point my gun at her and actually pull the trigger. I knew she'd kill me the first chance she got, but there was no way I could do it.

"So, how do you want to do this?" Darla swallowed her last sip.

"I don't."

"Would it be easier for you if I turned around?" Darla turned her back to me.

"Turn around."

"So you're not going to kill me?"

"I don't know, yet. You mind if I grab a glass of water?" I asked.

"Of course not."

I set my gun on the counter next to the sink and grabbed a glass from the cupboard. I turned on the faucet, filled the glass, and examined it before taking a drink. Then I poured it out and drank straight from the faucet. I didn't really think Darla had poisoned all her glasses, I was hoping she would reach for my gun while I was bent over the sink. I needed her to attack first. She did not.

"If you lived somewhere else, somewhere where your father couldn't protect you from the law, somewhere where you were the outsider, where you didn't feel the need to exterminate those that didn't fit the mold, would you need to kill?"

"I don't feel the need to kill anyone, now that I know Daddy's gone. I only did it because I was craving his approval." Her words were so sincere.

"If you promise to leave Lost Creek, right now, and never come back, I will walk out that door, right now. If you don't leave, I'll come back with Clancy. And I promise you he will not be so forgiving. And if I ever hear about any strange deaths in whatever town you settle, not only will I send your diary to every news organization I can think of, but, I promise you, I will hunt you down and kill you. You understand?"

"I understand."

"You promise?"

"I promise."

Darla's eyes shined soft and sincere. I actually believed she was going to skip town and never kill again as I turned and headed for the front door.

"I'll be back with Clancy in an hour. If we find you, or any evidence that you aren't keeping your word, I swear to you, we will hunt you down and kill you."

I was almost to the door when I heard that familiar metallic click of the safety. I slowly turned around to see Darla pointing Clancy's .9mm straight at my heart.

"You forget something?" Darla's smirk shined victoriously.

"Nope." I smiled as I pulled a handful of bullets from my pocket. I had unloaded the clip in my pocket before getting a drink of water.

Darla ejected the clip to find it empty. The look on her face told me she was more proud of my guile than angry at my deceit.

"Not bad, Jack, not bad."

My smile gleamed with righteousness as I slid Martin's knife from its leather holster. It was only right that I ended Darla's life with Martin's knife.

"You think you're so damn smart!" Darla violently jabbed the gun in my direction. BANG! Flames roared from the barrel. I can only imagine the look on my face was as riddled with surprise as Darla's as we studied the hole in the door no more than a few inches from my head. I had emptied the clip, but completely forgotten about the bullet in the chamber.

Darla threw the gun at my head and ran for the desk at the bottom of the stairs. I knew exactly what she was going for; I had seen a revolver in the top drawer while snooping one afternoon early in our relationship. I ran after her and tackled her just as she puller the revolver from the drawer. BANG! The gun blasted right next to my head. My ears were ringing as we sailed through the air and crashed into her glass coffee table. The impact knocked the gun from Darla's hand, but, somehow, she ended up on top of me, with her hands wrapped around my neck. Lying on a pile of broken glass, every time I tried to shift my weight to buck her off, the shards cut deeper into my back. She was like a rabid badger, grunting and squealing and choking the life from me. For such a little shit, she was surprisingly strong. It took both arms just to pry one of her hands from my throat. That turned out to be a mistake. As I tried to pull her other hand from my throat, Darla grabbed a long shard of glass and stabbed it for my throat. I stopped her just before the jagged tip punctured my skin. Her arm shook with such intensity the glass jabbed at my neck. Her hand was dripping with blood from her tight grip on the sharp shard. I couldn't breathe. And just as I started to get dizzy, I stopped trying to pry her hand from my throat. Darla smiled, thinking I had given up. The shard was just starting to sink into my throat when Darla realized I was reaching for my knife. It was too late. I plunged Martin's knife deep into her chest.

A strange look of relief washed over Darla's face as her warm scarlet stream flowed over my hand. That innocent glint once again sparkled in her eyes. For a brief second, she almost looked happy.

"I'm sorry," she gurgled before her lifeless body dropped on mine.

I was just about to shove Darla's bloody body off me when I caught our reflection in the mirror that hung high on the vaulted wall. At the awkward angle the mirror was hanging, our shattered-glass bloody mess looked almost beautiful. We were framed like a painting, lifeless yet vibrant, peaceful yet violent. Darla's scarlet pool slowly flowed till its shores surpassed the frame before I finally upset the scene.

I don't know what came over me in the moments that followed. I rushed around Darla's house like a madman trying to get rid of any evidence of my presence. It wasn't long before

I realized I couldn't possibly cover up the fact that something horrible had gone down. I thought I could make it look like Darla had fallen into the coffee table and it was the glass that had pierced her chest — I even jammed a piece of broken glass in the wound — then I realized the bullet hole in the door would not support such a theory. The next thing I knew, I was pouring gasoline all throughout the house. I placed a candle on the floor next to the busted coffee table. And I tossed a lit match into the entryway as I walked out.

The house exploded with flames that nearly blew me off my feet. I could still feel the heat when I climbed into my truck at the end of her driveway. The house was nothing but a smoldering pile of ash in less than an hour. The fire department never arrived. The entire fire department was manned by Campbells. The entire fire department was dead.

CHAPTER 11

Lost Creek was crawling with cops and reporters the very next day. Because Clancy had been shot, his shack burned down, and the fact that there were two dead Campbells found on his property, Clancy was thoroughly questioned. And because the cops found Clancy in my shack, they also brought me in for questioning. Clancy said they would. He told me to play dumb. I was to say nothing about knowing of the Campbell family secret. All I could tell them was that Clancy came stumbling onto my property, mumbling about the Campbells burning down his shack and shooting him. And that was all I told them. They really started grilling us by the second day. I had no idea what Clancy was telling them. But I was starting to get the feeling that we were their prime suspects. I was certain I would be spending the rest of my life in prison. Then, on the third day, the interrogations stopped and they released us. Darla's notebook had been delivered to the *Denver Post*'s mailbox. With Darla's house burned to the ground, the cops turned to the sheriff's home for clues. Betty had already heard the news. The cops found her hanging from the balcony railing when they arrived. They also found her cookbooks of death, along with a hand-drawn map locked away in a safe in the sheriff's study that led them to ninety-four bodies buried all around the county.

The final conclusion was that the sheriff's relatives had stumbled across the horrible things he and his family had been doing and the sheriff tried to kill them to cover it up. The cops never came back to question us. The reporters stopped knocking on my door after a couple weeks.

Spring was unbelievably peaceful after my winter debacle. Except that I was at Clancy and Blue's beck and call. It's hard to say which was the worse patient. Blue grumbled and groaned over the slightest noise. Clancy bitched about everything from the way I cooked his rabbit stew to the temperature of my shack. When the weather finally settled, I was more than happy to build Clancy a new shack — he supervised, constantly criticized, and played the "I'd do it myself if you hadn't shot me in the arm!" card the whole time.

I finished Clancy's shack, to Clancy's exact specifications, about a week ago. Blue has been back to his old self for at least a month — you would never know it if you saw him roll over, lick his scar, and beg for sympathy. He now does it every time he doesn't get his way. That dog plays the guilt card better than my mother.

And that brings us to this very day, exactly one year since I found myself adrift in Lost Creek. Had someone told me, on the day I first arrived, or for many months after, for that matter, that I would fall in love with this place, find myself, and never want to leave, I would have never believed. I could never have imagined living in such desolation. Living without a cell phone seemed barbaric. Forget about electricity and running water, I didn't think it was possible to live without the Internet. Now, I can't understand how anyone would willingly strap themselves to such absurdities. I couldn't possibly return to some city and plug myself into such chaos. But such realizations have brought just as much sorrow as joy. Martin has been on my mind for months. My mother flew out shortly after hearing on the national news that I was being questioned for murdering the Campbell family. It didn't take more than a few minutes in Martin's old shack before she admitted to the whole affair. The worst part, she hardly knew anything about Martin that Clancy hadn't already told me. I've spent many quiet nights this spring studying Martin's old maps and reading his Jack London book, over and over, trying to better understand the man I recently learned to be my father. I still don't know him.

That is why I have decided to embark on this next adventure. Blue and I are going to follow one of Martin's old maps and hike the Colorado Trail all the way to New Mexico and back. The round trip is over 1,200 miles, according to Martin's map. If I can keep his pace, it should take twelve weeks and three days. He marked everything on the map from how many miles to hike each day, how many hours the hike should take, where to camp, where to get water, and fishing spots; all the supplies needed for the trip are listed on the back of the map. My pack must weigh fifty pounds with all the supplies on Martin's list. It's going to be a tough pace to keep. Clancy says I better, and I better *not* get lost, or I won't have enough time to prepare for winter. He says it's going to be a brutal winter. He says he knows because the trees are storing their energy rather than promoting new growth. I think he's just trying to scare me into not leaving. To be honest with you, I almost hope I do get lost. For if this last year has taught me anything, it's that getting lost can be the best thing that can happen to a guy. Sometimes getting lost is the only way to find yourself.

ABOUT THE AUTHOR

Conceived in Colorado, born in Missouri, raised in Minnesota, R.j Ruud now resides high in the Rocky Mountains of Colorado where he spends his days skiing, snowboarding, hiking, biking, fishing, climbing, and camping—nights are for writing.
If you enjoyed Lost Creek, a good review on Amazon would be greatly appreciated. Connect on facebook/RjRuud